What Became of Her

BOOKS BY M.E. KERR

BLOOD ON THE FOREHEAD: *WHAT I KNOW ABOUT WRITING*
1999 Books for the Teen Age (The New York Public Library)

"HELLO," I LIED
1998 Books for the Teen Age (The New York Public Library)

DELIVER US FROM EVIE
1995 Best Books for Young Adults (ALA)
1995 Recommended Books for Reluctant Young Adult Readers (ALA)
1995 Fanfare Honor List (The Horn Book)
1995 Books for the Teen Age (The New York Public Library)
1994 School Library Journal *Best Books of the Year*
1994 Booklist *Books for Youth Editors' Choices*
1994 Best Book Honor (Michigan Library Association)

LINGER
1994 Book for the Teen Age (The New York Public Library)

NIGHT KITES
1991 California Young Reader Medal
Best of the Best Books (YA) 1966–1986 (ALA)
1987 Recommended Book for Reluctant Young Adult Readers (ALA)
Booklist's *Best of the '80s*

FELL DOWN
1991 Booklist *Books for Youth Editors' Choices*
1992 Books for the Teen Age (The New York Public Library)

FELL BACK

1990 Edgar Allan Poe Award Finalist (Mystery Writers of America)
1990 Books for the Teen Age (The New York Public Library)

FELL

1987 Best Books for Young Adults (ALA)
1987 Booklist Books for Youth Editors' Choices
1988 Books for the Teen Age (The New York Public Library)

LITTLE LITTLE

1981 School Library Journal Best Books of the Year
1981 Golden Kite Award (SCBWI)
1982 Books for the Teen Age (The New York Public Library)

GENTLEHANDS

Best of the Best Books (YA) 1966–1992 (ALA)
1978 School Library Journal Best Books of the Year
1978 Christopher Award
1978 Outstanding Children's Books of the Year (The New York Times)
1979 Books for the Teen Age (The New York Public Library)

IF I LOVE YOU, AM I TRAPPED FOREVER?

1973 Outstanding Children's Books of the Year (The New York Times)
1973 Child Study Association's Children's Books of the Year
1973 Book World's Children's Spring Book Festival Honor Book

DINKY HOCKER SHOOTS SMACK!

Best of the Best Books (YA) 1970–1983 (ALA)
1972 Notable Children's Book (ALA)
1972 School Library Journal Best Books of the Year
Children's Books of 1972 (Library of Congress)

What Became of Her

A NOVEL BY

M. E. KERR

HARPERCOLLINS*PUBLISHERS*

"Passing a Truck Full of Chickens at Night on Highway Eighty"
on pages 96–97 is reprinted from *The Lord and the General Din of the World*,
by Jane Mead, published by Sarabande Books, Inc. © 1996 by Jane Mead.
Reprinted by permission of Sarabande Books and the author.

The lines on page 90 are from "Fate" by Fanny Heaslip Lea,
copyright 1920, Meredith Corporation. Courtesy of *Ladies' Home Journal*.

Library of Congress Cataloging-in-Publication Data
Kerr, M. E.
    What became of her : a novel / M. E. Kerr
        p.   cm.
    Summary: Edgar Tobbit meets Neal Kraft at a group session arranged by their
psychotherapist and their friendship ends up thwarting the plans of an eccentric widow
to get revenge on the town where she was mistreated as a young girl.
    ISBN 0-06-028435-8. — ISBN 0-06-028436-6 (lib. bdg.)
    [1. Revenge—Fiction.   2. Interpersonal relations—Fiction.]   I. Title.
PZ7.K46825 Wg   2000   99-052656
[Fic]—dc21   CIP
                                                                                    AC

Typography by Matt Adamec   1 2 3 4 5 6 7 8 9 10   ❖   First Edition

This book is for my two handsome brothers:
Charlie Meaker in Arizona
and
Ellis Meaker in California

What Became of Her

—from *THE SERENITY BANNER*
SUNDAY BOOK SECTION

INTERVIEWER: In your book you call your main character Rosalind Slaymaster. We know her by another name, of course. How did you find out so much about her?
AUTHOR: I came upon her diaries, some letters, and her scrapbook. Then, too, for a very short time, I knew her. . . . I begin my book with the night I met her. Only the names are changed.

One

Out of the blue one winter day, Rosalind Slaymaster asked my mother and me to dinner. The reason for the invitation was a mystery to us.

Mrs. Slaymaster had restored the old Evans house, up on Canal Cliffs. It used to have another name: Evans Above.

That was changed, as the house was.

Peligro, the sign said. *Danger*—because the road that led up to the house twisted sharply around the hill.

One of the Hispanic workers had made the sign as the house was being prepared for its new owner. When Rosalind Slaymaster was finally ready to live there, everyone in town had come to call the place Peligro.

In the town of Serenity, they said it was like her to leave it that way.

❄   ❄   ❄

Rosalind Slaymaster sat at the head of the table that night. I was seated at the other end, facing her.

She was said to be the richest woman in Bucks County, Pennsylvania. She didn't look rich, not then and not when I'd see her around town. But it didn't take very long after talking with her to realize that she wasn't just like anyone else, either. It wasn't only because she had piles of money. It was the toughness of her, the hard twang in her voice, and this walk she had like she was Boss of Everywhere.

She looked and acted more Texan than Eastern. But she'd been born in Serenity, the last one anyone ever thought would come back to lord it over everybody. She still lived most of the time on The Lucky Star, her ranch near Ingram, Texas.

Next to me my mother perched excitedly on the edge of her cushioned chair. On the other side of me sat Mrs. Slaymaster's niece, Julie, age fifteen, a year younger than I was. Red Brillo hair. Thick glasses. Beside Julie was the *real* star of Peligro. Named for a preacher who'd baptized Mrs. Slaymaster's late husband, he was called Peale.

Peale was not a person, not an animal, but a large leather doll, dressed that evening in a black suit with a bolo tie, a black silk vest with silver threads, and black suede boots.

My mother was as nervous as a dog that knows a thunderstorm's on the way. Everything about Peligro, from its 10,000 square feet (five bedrooms, seven bathrooms) to its imperious owner, was too rich for my mother's blood.

There had been very little conversation through the soup course. Two teenagers who hardly know each other don't promise dynamite dialogue. Mrs. S., as everyone called her, seemed content to eat in silence. I had an idea they didn't talk much at the table, company or not. You know those couples you see out in restaurants sometimes who aren't saying boo to each other unless one needs the salt? I figured that was probably the way *they* were.

Mom made too much of everything: showering compliments on the meal, on the crystal chandelier hanging from the thirty-foot ceiling, on the white brick fireplace at the end of the dining room, even on the chairs we sat on. Anything she could toss in. She was overwhelmed.

Finally, desperately, after a long silence, she cleared her throat.

She said importantly, "They say I was royalty in another life."

It wasn't the first time I'd heard it. Mom really believed it, and she resorted to mentioning it times she felt outclassed.

Mrs. Slaymaster did not even look up from her plate. "Who are *they*?" she asked.

"Those who know about spiritual things," my mother replied. "Those who make a study of reincarnation." Mom was little and thin, making me always afraid someone would treat her in a way that would diminish her further.

Mrs. Slaymaster roared, "Cow pie!"

"I beg your pardon?" my mother said, red-faced.

"I don't buy into that crap, Ann!"

"But what is 'cow pie'?"

"*Merde*," Julie spoke up. "*Merde* from a moo cow."

"Number two," I whispered, knowing Mom knew no French.

Mrs. S. said, "We get one crack at life, Ann! We go around one time."

"*One Life to Live*," Julie put in, pushing her eyeglasses back on her nose. "There used to be a soap called that."

"Is that what you learned to do in your boarding schools?" Mrs. S. asked. "Watch television soap operas?"

"It's what I learned to do in Texas, Aunt. It's what you do when there's no one around for miles and miles and miles. You resort to the boob tube."

My mother, a world-class viewer of soaps, Rosie—Oprah—all of it—blushed again and offered the information that *I* rarely watched anything on TV.

"Good for you, Edward." Mrs. S. looked across at me, almost smiling. I had an idea a smile didn't come easily to those lips.

"Edgar," Julie corrected her. "But he's called E.C."

Like Peale, I, too, had been named for someone. Edgar Cayce, a psychic of some importance in that far-out world of crystal balls and Ouija boards.

A young man in a white coat came from the kitchen to clear.

When he had finished, and set down a chocolate cake with plates and a knife, Mrs. S. glanced up at him. "*Gracias*, Paulo."

Paulo didn't acknowledge the thanks from Mrs. S. He, too, looked as though smiling was about as natural to him as embroidering.

Dessert was dished out by the lady of the house. That was when she told us her reason for inviting us to dinner, or at least the reason my mother had been asked there.

She leaned back in her chair, resting her arms on its mahogany sides, and said to my mother, "Although I consider most occult things malarkey, astrology amuses me."

"I happen to draw up astrological charts!" my mother said proudly.

"I know that, Ann. I've seen your ads in the local paper. That's why you're here."

"Would you like me to do your chart?"

"Not mine. How would you like to do a chart for P-E-A-L-E?"

My mother frowned. "The doll?"

Mrs. S. put her finger to her lips. "*Shhh*. We never refer to him that way, Ann. I spelled his name because I want it to be a surprise for him."

"I'm sorry, Mrs. Slaymaster."

9

"He's a remarkable creature who can grant wishes and make dreams come true. I'm never without him. He goes wherever I go. He even has his own passport."

"And his own wardrobe," Julie said. "He has dozens of handmade shoes, and he has thirty-two tailor-made suits."

"We don't announce that, Julie. That makes us look prodigal."

I wasn't sure what "prodigal" meant, but what Mrs. Slaymaster looked like to me was a character out of the old West—a tall cowboy in bright-red lipstick. I had never seen her out of jeans, but then I had never seen her anywhere except on the streets of Serenity. She usually wore leather boots with the jeans, leather vests, old caps perched on her silver, cropped hair. She had pale-green eyes, a big mouth, and big white teeth. She didn't just walk down a street. She took it over. She swaggered.

She said, "Well, Ann? What about it? I'll pay top price."

"But I have to know things like the exact time of birth, or *creation*, the place, and—"

"I have all the vital statistics, Ann."

Peale was standing up in his chair. He was a stuffed leather mannequin with leather ears and black hair. About two feet tall, he was almost the same height as Rosalind Slaymaster was sitting.

My mother broke the silence in her quiet, sweet tones, announcing that she would be happy to do Peale's chart.

She even remembered to spell out his name.

"Hooray!" Mrs. S. exclaimed. I could see it took some effort for her to sound jovial. "That takes care of his birthday. He came into this world on Christmas Eve. I always throw a small party before I *adios* this place and head home for New Year's. Why don't you two come?"

"Christmas Eve is my birthday, too," said my mother.

"Then you have to come! Oh, yes, you must. And bring someone if you want." She turned to me then. "You, too, E.C. You bring someone, too. A girl, a buddy, or fly solo."

"What a nice invitation!" my mother said. "Thank you!"

I didn't have to ask my mother who she'd invite.

The only good thing about the shrink she'd started dating was that I didn't have to go to him anymore.

Two

Last April, when he was still my shrink, Darwin C. Duke announced that it was time for me to go from individual therapy to group.

"And talk about my feelings with kids from school? No way."

"Way," he said. "These kids are all grieving for a parent, a brother, or a sister. This is a closure group. It will give you a sense of connection and help you deal with your isolation."

"I don't feel that isolated."

"You don't seem to have many friends."

"I don't have *any*. It's got nothing to do with Dad's death. I'm just a loner, same as he was."

"He may have been a loner, but he wasn't alone. He had your mother, and he had you. . . . You may talk about whatever you want to talk about in group. You can dump on us, if you want, or you can keep it light."

I talked about my ex, Arden.

Dr. Duke would suggest that I was *displacing*. Tackling a smaller pain to avoid the larger one.

But the two had happened one after the other.

My father's death, expected . . . Arden's desertion, unexpected.

The others would laugh out loud after I'd begin my spiel by saying, "And here is something else about The Beautiful But Very Evil Arden Cutler."

It got so I began to think maybe I should forget about being a writer or a photojournalist and just become a stand-up comic.

There was one kid who didn't laugh out loud. He didn't laugh, period. His name was Neal Kraft.

Neal was known for his dancing. At SHS dances everybody'd stop at some point just to watch him. No girl he was with could move like he could. Neal was a natural. Plus he had been taught every dance from the Charleston to the tango by his dance-instructor mother.

He was two grades ahead of me, so I didn't know him well.

But boys *didn't* know Neal well. Boys didn't like him. The kind of people who liked Neal were female.

I remembered his father, though. We all remembered him. That was the other thing Neal was known for besides dancing: his father's suicide.

Perry Kraft was older than most of our fathers.

Everybody'd been surprised, because it was said you could go into Kraft Drugs with anything from a boil to rheumatoid arthritis, and Mr. Kraft would welcome you with a smile, sit you down, and suggest ways to help you. Nobody ever figured that *he* needed help.

One day, group was dragging. Judy Proust had brought in a tape of an old Mariah Carey song called "One Sweet Day." She said if Mariah Carey had not written that song, she would probably have swallowed her father's sleeping pills and joined her mother in the great beyond.

It was some song.

Nearly all of our eyes were full. No one could think of anything to say.

I decided it was time for a little comic relief.

If I didn't laugh about Arden Cutler, I'd cry.

My dad used to play an old jazz record called "I Was in Love With a Thirsty Woman Who Drank My Tears." That was my story put to music.

"I will never forget this night as long as I live"—I liked to start off with a grabber. "I call it 'The Night of the Phish Food Surprise' . . . orrrrrrrr: 'Just one more example of my heart's trials at the hands of The Beautiful But Very Evil Arden Cutler.'"

I explained how much I had always admired the Sigma

Epsilon Delta fraternity ring that lay in my father's sock drawer. When I told him once I wouldn't mind having it, he said he only kept it to remind himself what a stuffy little pisser he'd been in college. He said he'd give it to me, but it wouldn't be appropriate to wear a fraternity ring if you weren't one of the "brothers." Then he added, "I hope you'll never become one. They're just holier-than-thous sitting around by candlelight in their cashmere sweaters deciding who to blackball. . . . Anyway," he went on, "it looks like a girl's ring. Who wears a gold ring with a little diamond on black ebony?"

She would wear it, I told myself when I was emptying that drawer after his death. Arden would love it . . . and I wouldn't tell her why my father'd kept it.

Arden's favorite ice cream was Ben & Jerry's Phish Food, which I brought over to her house on a Saturday night when her parents gave us the living room, while they took over the den.

While Arden found a movie for us to watch among the dozens of cable options piped into the Cutler house, I went into the kitchen. I put the ring in the bottom of her dish of Phish Food.

"What is this?" she said when it finally appeared out of the chocolate fog, a little wet sparkler looking important enough to shake itself off and sing the SED fraternity song. "We ought to fax Ben & Jerry and tell them we're going to sue if they don't settle something on us! It looks like a bottle top to me!"

"Honey, it's not a bottle top."

And that was the point in my story when Neal Kraft lost it.

He began shouting. "Last Fourth of July I cut my father down from a beam in the back of his store, his eyes like the eyes of a fish on the end of a hook and he'd whizzed in his pants. . . . Do I care about some asshole Mariah Carey song? Or about some moron who stuck a diamond in chocolate ice cream, do you think?"

Silence.

"You see what you've done again, Neal?" said Doctor Duke. "You've tried to manipulate the group."

Finally, Neal looked across at me and said, "Go on, Tobbit. Let's hear your tragic little story."

So I did the dialogue anyway, just to prove that he wasn't going to manipulate *me*.

—Maybe if you just scoop it out of the sauce and pick it up.

—It's too yucky, E.C.

—It's my father's fraternity ring, Arden.

—I could never take your ring unless I was in love with you.

—What do you mean unless you were in love with me?

—Sometimes you love someone you're not in love with.

Eeeeek, it's goopy, don't get it near my pants, hon. These are DKNYs.

—I'll wash it off.

—Sit back down. E.C.? Have you heard me mention Nelson Marland?

Then I said, "To be continued. . . ."

Once again, everyone laughed but Neal.

Later that afternoon I was browsing around Bookworm, this swank new store next to my mother's hair salon, Crowning Glory. I'd hang out in their leather armchairs when I was waiting for a ride home with Mom.

I was looking at magazines when I spotted Neal. I had to hand it to him: He had a certain style. He was standing there, wearing an RAF leather bomber jacket with a white silk scarf. His back was to me. He was going through the CD sale rack, holding a Rufus Wainwright album in one hand and a Stephen King book in the other.

Neal looked a little like Wainwright. He had the same black hair, the same brooding boyishness. He wore a small gold ring on his right ear.

I watched him stand there looking from his right hand to his left, as though he didn't know which to buy. I was going to tell him not to bother with *Skeleton Crew* because King wasn't at his best writing short stories. That was before I knew how much Neal read, that Neal knew more about

King than I did, and that King was his god!

I was just about to amble over his way when, quick as a wink, he slid the King book under his jacket.

Then he turned around and saw me.

I said, "Hi."

"You," he said. He walked closer to me.

"Yeah, me. Why are King's books so long?"

"I have a theory about that," Neal said. "I think it's because he's just as compelled as all the mad characters he creates. He's also a schizo. He's got that other name he writes under, Richard Bachman. If he didn't write, he'd do sinister stuff, you know? He'd be roaming around with a long knife. Do you agree, E.C.?"

"Or maybe he's just a ham, an egomaniac. He can't get off the stage."

"He's not a narcissist, if that's what you're saying. He makes his lead characters too sensitive . . . like the writer in *Bag of Bones*. The hell with some sentimental Mariah Carey song. You read about that guy talking about missing his wife after her death, and that's where it's at!"

I agreed.

I always liked the way Stephen King started out. In every book I'd ever read of his, there'd be this cool beginning and you couldn't help getting hooked. Then pretty soon stuff would happen that was more in my mother's area of expertise. My brain had its own little nut shop relentlessly presenting me with dilemmas, like go back and see if the porch door is locked after I've been back to see if it's locked four times in a row, and why couldn't I stop saying over and over to myself, *He's not around, he's in the ground*?

But I was not that receptive to other people's nut-shop shows, so it was hard reading about King's talking cars and refrigerator magnets that spelled out *Help r*. I was happier with George V. Higgins, Elmore Leonard, and Robert Cormier.

Neal was taller than I was. At five feet ten I was your typical blond blah boy. Okay-looking but you'd see me everywhere in crowds, at malls, on sitcoms.

Arden had wanted me to grow a little chin beard, or get an ear pierced. She'd said I could use some style. She wanted me to look more like one of those preppies in Polo ads pouting down by his canoe with his coat collar turned up and his hair tangled.

When we got outside, Neal looked me in the eye. "It's not like taking something that belongs to somebody. I wouldn't take anything from a local store, but Bookworm is a chain like the A&P. Who cares if you cheat the A&P out of a few nickels?"

Among my mother's superstitions was the one about stealing. When you stole from someone, you stole the person's bad luck along with what you were taking. I didn't know how it worked when you swiped something from someplace like the A&P. Maybe your refrigerator freezer would break down and all your food would thaw. Or maybe someone would take a dive on your front sidewalk and sue you for a permanent back injury.

"I'm curious," Neal said. "When The Beautiful But Very Evil Arden Cutler dumped you, did she say she'd confused *like* and *love*? She liked you but she didn't love you? Or she loved you but she didn't like you?"

"Close," I said.

"It's what they do," he said. "That's where you were headed in group, wasn't it? Girls never just say they don't know why they've lost the feeling. They get psychosemantic. They start analyzing everything they felt from the time you first met. Why do you suppose girls do that?"

I said, "I didn't even think you were listening to me in group."

"Hey, I heard every word you said. You're the only one who's not wallowing in his own *merde*."

"Besides you," I laughed, and Neal nodded and slapped my back.

Neal smoked these strange, little brown Indian cigarettes called bidis. He preferred the strawberry-flavored ones, which he drove twenty-six miles to Doylestown to buy. He lit one and asked me where I was going.

That was how we ended up next door, where my dog,

Doon, was waiting near the hair dryers for a walk. We took him all over Serenity, talking about everything.

I could not stop myself from liking Neal. Maybe what I admired most about him was the way he asked me what I thought about things, his eyes watching me when I answered, with an earnestness that seemed to imply he might actually change his mind about something because of what I'd said. Clearly he would think over things we had discussed. That was something I thought I'd never have again, after Dad's death.

I told myself, So what if he takes stuff? On the important issues he felt the same way I did. Both of us hated it that Dutchman Park was soon going to be renamed Sonny Fitch Park. It had been Dutchman for 150 years, a good-enough name for generations of kids who hung out there summers.

Rosalind Slaymaster was paying to have the place overhauled, but only if they'd name it after her father.

"Who *cares* about her old man?" Neal said.

"She thinks she owns this town," I said.

"She's not far wrong about that," said Neal.

Back then I'd never set eyes on Mrs. Slaymaster.

I hadn't even discussed her with anyone, or told a soul how it bugged me that she could buy anything she wanted to in Serenity, even the name of one of its favorite places.

I'd never had a pal or been a talker. But Neal and I hit it off right away. He seemed so easy. . . . Funny, too, that before the afternoon was over, he'd stopped calling me E.C. and nicknamed me Easy.

Three

In our school it seemed to be an unwritten law that if you were new, you had to wait for acceptance. You were like some animal at the pound waiting to be adopted. You couldn't take it for granted.

It was easier if you were a boy, because you'd be thrown on some team that would need you to win. Boys' sports were big in Serenity, Pa., but the girls didn't have a reason to need anyone, particularly this clique who called themselves The Sluts.

The Sluts lived in their own little world, and maybe they would and maybe they wouldn't stop huddling together someday to smile at you.

Julie seemed doomed from the beginning. She came to us in November, fresh from being booted out of a New England boarding school. We'd all gone to school together since kindergarten. She arrived from Peligro every morning in this gross white Hummer, with Mrs. S. at the wheel.

Julie reminded me of a silly puppy crashing on wobbly legs into the midst of a pack of full-grown, disgruntled dogs, neither surprised nor discouraged by their snarls and growls. And like a puppy, it didn't appear to register with her how welcome she wasn't.

After that dinner at Peligro I kept a watchful eye out for Julie. In my heart the PROTECT button was sounding like the END buzzer in our microwave. My button buzzed for deer done out of their woods by developers, dogs tied to trees under the hot sun, calves that spent their lives in cages for diners who fancied veal, and occasionally for a two-footed wretch as well. This was a legacy from my father, who'd saved feral cats, wounded critters, woodlands, and wetlands—saved everything but money.

I waited for Julie one afternoon at the end of last bell.

"I'll walk you home. I need the exercise." Exercise was one thing I didn't need. Every morning, way early, I hiked from my house to a general store, where my job was to prepare newspapers for delivery.

I took the books from her arms.

The most noticeable thing about Julie was this wild mop of red hair. It sat atop her head like the dialogue balloon over the heads in comics. She had a large butterfly-shaped collection of freckles under both eyes and across the bridge of her nose. Sliding down that nose was a black plastic Gucci frame with square lenses tinted gray-green.

Julie was a spiller, my mother's name for clients who spilled out every detail of their personal life while she did their hair. By the time we got to Old Ferry Road, Julie had told me that when she was four years old, a speedboat her mother was riding in hit a rock in the Guadalupe River and exploded.

"She'd been drinking martinis," she continued. "She was stinking drunk. It was in all the newspapers. My poor mama was this wild thing. Smoke what's around, swallow what's around, drink what's around. The hell with watching me grow up."

"That's rough, Julie. I'm sorry."

"I used to be so sorry too, because I imagined this dude with a scythe—Death—just cutting her down in her prime. But now I know that dude doesn't have to do boo for certain people. He just waits. They do it to themselves just like they jumped off a roof or stepped in front of a train. I even wrote something about it for your school essay contest."

"It's your school too, now."

"I don't last places, Eddie. I could be sent to prison and they'd find some reason to ship me back before I'd served my time. . . . Aunt says it's because I'm so hungry for friends, I'm like an urchin at a garden party—I just embarrass people and make them uncomfortable. Do you think I do that, Eddie?"

"No . . . and no one calls me Eddie."

"You know what my mother's name was?" she said. "Crystal Calldownthemoon. She grew up in this all-female goddess commune down in the panhandle."

"What happened to your father?"

"What father?"

"Okay."

She could rattle on and on without seeming to take a breath.

"Aunt's not my real aunt. I don't think I have any real relatives."

"You get along okay with Mrs. Slaymaster?" I asked. I had a feeling she didn't. How do you get along okay with someone who tells you that you embarrass people and make them uncomfortable?

"I just wish her idea of home wasn't a six-hundred-fifty-acre ranch plunked down in the middle of nowhere," Julie said. "Right outside the door any day you can find one or all four of the deadliest snakes in the U. S. of A. Copperheads, water moccasins, rattlesnakes, and coral snakes. But now she *says* we're going to try living up here. She has a big thing about this town."

"So they say." I'd heard that the "big thing" was a chip on her shoulder the size of *Apollo 11*.

"Of course she *claims* she's coming back here because she wants me to go to Chalfont my last two years of high. She says I need tone."

"You might like being a Chaly." I doubted it. Chalfont was a private school in Serenity. Chaly girls would make The Sluts look like the Girl Scouts. Next stop for a Chaly was Harvard, Yale, Vassar, some Ivy League lockup. It was the type of school with an Ancestors' Club, automatic membership if your great-great-aunt Laura graduated from there.

Julie looked over at me and out of nowhere said, "Do you see a shrink?"

"Why do you ask?" Answer a question with a question. That ought to tell her something. Doctor, why do I think Dad can see my every move now? *Why do you think you think that, E.C.?*

"I feel like I'm on a couch babbling away," Julie said.

"I see a shrink three or four times a week. Sometimes more."

"Oh, man, Eddie! What's wrong with you?" But she had this little grin, as though the idea of me being a major sicko was a plus.

I had to dash her hopes of hanging out with a basket case.

"A certain Doctor Darwin Duke dates my mother." I still had trouble with the idea of "date" and "my mother" in the same sentence. And The Duck wasn't irresistible, either. I'd promised Mom I wouldn't call him that, but I knew I was on the verge of slipping again, because I had an appreciative audience.

"Your *Mom* dates your *shrink*?"

"He *was* my shrink. First I saw him one on one. Then I was in a group until my mother was late picking me up one day. He came out of his office just as she arrived, and ever since he's been more interested in her than me. She doesn't have to pay for it, either."

"So he's in your house all the time?"

"Not *all* the time. Just Wednesday nights. Just Friday nights. Most Saturday nights. Sundays. They both like to dance. They go out to dinner places they can dance. The Duck is short and so's Mom."

"I thought you said his name was Duke."

"Duck's my affectionate name for him. What does the duck say?"

Julie laughed. "Quack quack," she said.

Four

Every year the winner of the SHS Essay Contest for freshmen and sophomores was announced at a party in the gym. The judges didn't know whose essay it was until they awarded the prizes: $500 for the best essay, $300 for the runner-up, and $100 each for third and fourth places.

I decided to write something about Dutchman Park. There was some momentum building among the Don't Ditch Dutchman crowd, who weren't convinced it was a done deal. There were buttons saying "Go Dutch" and graffiti everywhere blasting the name Sonny Fitch.

This essay wasn't going to be "lyrical"—the word my freshman English teacher used to describe a piece I'd written for class about None Other Than. I'd even used Arden's real name. I'd say that to myself nights I couldn't sleep and was thrashing around in bed thinking of every horrible thing

I'd ever done. Using her real name in that essay was way up there at the top of the list. I'd groan in the dark, "How could I have used Arden's real name!"

I'd hear her saying, "Honey, I love you but I was never *in love* with you."

Besides Patsy Persea, I liked to think I was the best writer in tenth grade. She had an advantage over me because she traveled all over the world with her family, and she wrote these essays entitled "The Gypsies of Dresden," or "Elba—Napoleon's Island." Tough competition when I was usually writing about somewhere I'd never been and, as it turned out, someone I never knew.

The night after I walked Julie home from school, I was parked on the living-room couch working on the essay while my mother sat at the card table across from me doing Peale's chart. She was looking things up in books, making notes, clicking her calculator, and hitting the keys on her laptop.

I finally said, "You're not really going to all that trouble for a doll?"

"He's a very interesting doll," my mother said. "He's going to travel, that much is clear."

"Mom?"

"What, sweetheart?"

"Do you think Mrs. Slaymaster remembers you from the past?"

"No. My name is Tobbit now, for one thing, and your dad wasn't from around here. But Rose—she wasn't Rosalind then—Rose and I never even spoke. I was younger, and I had my own crowd. Rose didn't belong anywhere."

"Was it *that* bad?"

"It was worse than bad. When you're older and you look back, you don't know why you didn't *do* something when someone was treated so unfairly. Why didn't we try to stop the bullies?"

"Stop them from doing what?"

My mother took her hands off the laptop and looked at me. "Rose stuttered. The kids called her Ro Ro, and sometimes they sang 'Row Row Row Your Boat,' because she'd say her name was Ro Ro Rose.

"Cornelius Kraft and his lackeys would hide in the bushes, jump out and hold her, then pull her sweater and bra off and throw it up in the trees. She always had a very large bust for a girl her age. She'd run home flame faced, and the kids would be laughing." My mother's face had turned red too.

"Was Cornelius Kraft from Neal's family?"

"Neal was named after him. He'd be Neal's uncle if he'd lived."

"Go on."

"Rose and her father lived over the garage at Dare's Funeral Home," Mom continued. "Rose had been born to two adults from '85.'"

"I thought everyone at 85 Havens Avenue was retarded."

"That was the word they used back then, yes. Rose was an accident. Her mother died giving birth, and Sonny—her father—everyone called him Sonny, even Rose—was always trying to find a way they could live together, because almost immediately Rose was put in Tall Trees, the orphanage. Then the Dares took them both in.

"Kids would go by on their bikes and shout at Sonny, 'Hey, Corpse Cleaner,' because it was said besides doing yard work and keeping the hearse and flower cars shined up, he did that work, too. Washed the bodies. And Rose helped him, they said. Rose put on the makeup and did the hair. You can imagine what kids could make of that, E.C."

"Kids are not a kindly breed, are we, Mom?"

"That's enough, honey. I don't want to get into a negative thought flow, E.C. I've got my hands full with Peale."

"What do you see there, Mom? You're shaking your head like you see bad stuff."

I could tell from the look in her eyes she was going to ignore the leather reality of her new client. A privileged relationship was a privileged relationship, never mind that it was like guarding the secrets of a shoe or a belt. She said, "Why don't you just concentrate on your homework? What are you studying?"

"English." I didn't tell her I was writing an essay against

the Dutchman Park name change. My mother was from the school of Don't Make Waves, just the opposite of Dad. Anyway, I wasn't a spiller. Mom was lucky that way. All day at her beauty shop she'd hear a mixture of gossip, regret, braggadocio, and longing, but she came home to The Sphinx.

Times she went out with Doctor Duke, she sometimes got tested. He'd ask her to do things like draw a house and then tell her all the smoke coming out of her chimney meant she was a warm person. Mom laughed when I asked her if there wasn't a better way of finding that out than making someone draw on the tablecloth, but she never let me go too far criticizing him.

Sometimes the doctor made Mom mad when he'd get on her case about all the spiritual stuff. He'd either make fun of it or try to disprove it. They had a real on-again, off-again relationship. Not off-again enough to suit me.

When the phone rang, I let Mom answer it. The bell no longer tolled for me, now that Arden was out of my life. I knew who was tolling the bell, too. I couldn't stand their conversations, or the way she'd chuckle. I couldn't believe my mother would actually laugh at anything *he'd* say.

I'd ache for Dad.

I headed for my room, our Airedale, Doon, following me.

My dad had tried everything to live: prayer, radiation, chemotherapy, pills, and even, toward the end, my mother's hocus-pocus: herbs and chanting, on and on. What he had valued, Crystal Calldownthemoon and Perry Kraft had tossed to the winds like a piece of used Kleenex.

I flopped on my bed and Doon leaped up to lick my face, then bury his nose under the pillow next to me. He had a thing for pillows. He'd hide under them, mostly, his back end sticking out. But sometimes he'd growl at one, knock it to the floor, then grab it with his teeth and shake it. We'd come home sometimes and find a pile of feathers.

"One of Doon's imaginary dragons," Dad would say.

Maybe it didn't matter, I thought, what you did or didn't do in life. Maybe we were just the pillows of some higher power who made us into dragons on a whim.

There we were, then there we weren't.

Five

"Your mom told my mom you were at Evans Above the other night," Neal said.

"Peligro."

"That's right. Now it's Peligro."

Neal had been waiting for me by the front door at school. He had on a red fez with a black tassel, and an SHS basketball team sweater. He said, "Yesterday I saw Mrs. Slaymaster in her Hummer at a railroad crossing with that dummy next to her in a child seat. The crossbars were lowered, and the train was chugging by. She sat there leaning on her horn, cussing away."

"That sounds like her."

"What's Peligro like?"

"It's big, and modern. Neal? Why don't you come there with me on Christmas Eve."

I told him about the party, and the invitation from Mrs. S. to bring anyone I wanted to.

"I have to partner Mom in her dance recital."

Mrs. Kraft had inherited Top Hat from her mother, but Neal had convinced her that name was too old-fashioned. Now it was called KDS, for Kraft Dance Studio.

"Come as soon as you can," I told Neal.

"Okay! I will! How about doing something in the library for me?" Neal said. "Mr. Rossi says if I organize the holiday decorating, I can quit the band. I'm a lousy musician, Easy—I want outa there!"

"What do I have to do?"

"Just go to the library and wrap some packages. They're for display under the Christmas tree. You'd really be helping me out, Easy."

Anything I wrapped looked like a gorilla'd done it, but after last bell I went down to the library and did the best I could. Three of us took these boxes and put this red paper with white trees on some, and white paper with red trees on others. The red and white bows we attached were already tied.

Then I walked down to the village and into Crowning Glory.

Under the dryer sat the woman who called Bingo at Holy Family. My mother was giving our next-door neighbor a cut. The television wasn't on, which meant she'd had a lot of customers. "Clients" she called them.

The Butler sisters were in the process of leaving: Mildred and Marilyn, who went everywhere together and ran Toybucks, the local children's store. They were searching for Mildred's cashmere scarf, which Marilyn bet was stolen.

"Hi, honey!" Mom said.

"Busy day, hmmm?"

"Rush, rush, rush," Mom said.

"Well, don't rush with me," our neighbor said. "Whenever you rush, you thin me out too much, Ann."

Doon was sacked out on his pillow under the cash register. I took him for a walk, cutting it short when I saw him shivering. He'd never liked the cold. He'd shake his paws when they hit snow. What Doon liked to do in winter was stay indoors and chew up things. Doon liked to do that in any season.

The Butler sisters were leaving just as I slipped Doon through the door.

"She found your scarf because she's psychic," Mildred whispered to Marilyn.

"Or psycho," said Marilyn, giggling. "If you ask me, she's got one oar out of the water."

A lot of my mother's "clients" pretended things my mother said while she did their hair weren't that unusual, then bent double laughing at her once they got out in the street.

37

Dad used to say that there are those of us who can't forgive certain others for not being ourselves.

I gave the Butler sisters the finger behind their backs, and scowled my way down toward the bus stop.

But I had to smile when I went through the parking lot.

There was the white Hummer.

Peale was sitting up front, wearing dark glasses in a white frame. There was a white wool scarf tied around his neck, and he was wearing red earmuffs.

For some reason I went over to the car and tried the door.

Of course, Mrs. Slaymaster had locked it. Peale was safe from harm. I should have known she wouldn't leave him unprotected, but I couldn't help imagining what a state she'd be in if somone had just reached in and taken him.

Already I was beginning to think of Peale as human, the way everyone at Peligro did.

Six

I can remember when the SHS Essay Contest was called The Christmas Essay. After some parents objected to that, it became The Christmas/Chanukah Essay. When petitions circulated suggesting it be renamed the Christmas/Chanukah/ Kwanzaa Essay, it was just named for the school.

Before the winners were announced, we stood and sang the school song encouraging us to fight on for SHS, as though we were all in bunkers on a battlefield in a foreign land, unlikely to make it home for Christmas, Chanukah, or Kwanzaa.

Then Mr. Rossi, the school principal, announced the winning writers, beginning with fourth place. Meredith Merola won with her description of a Christmas in Costa Rica.

Third was Patsy Persea for a piece called "The View From Tryvannshogda," about standing on a hill in Norway.

I won the $300 for second place with my essay, "Don't Ditch Dutchman!"

"And last, but certainly not least, we have our winner," said Mr. Rossi. "The essay is as original as its title, which is 'Dude With a Scythe.' . . . And the winner is Julie Slaymaster! Our heartfelt congratulations, Julie, for your words of wisdom."

Copies of the essay were passed out as a blushing Julie went up to the podium to accept her check and the huge brass fountain pen with SHS embossed on one side, Julie's name on the other.

There was the rattle of paper in the background. No one could believe Julie had won. No one could wait to read something with that wacky title.

I could see why it had won favor with the judges. It was about Julie's rage at Crystal Calldownthemoon, as well as a knock at young stars like Kurt Cobain and River Phoenix, who thought they could win a race with the dude with a scythe.

It was telling kids you have to pay your dues no matter who you are.

I didn't think kids wanted to hear that kind of lecture from another kid . . . particularly a kid from Peligro who arrived at school every morning in a white Hummer. I didn't think they wanted to hear any lecture at all from someone connected with the renaming of Dutch.

When a toothy trio finished singing "This Old Man," I tapped Julie on the shoulder and said, "Congratulations!"

She said, "I never thought I'd *win* the thing!"

"Oh, my, yes, Julie," Patsy Persea cooed, leaning forward in the row, several seats away from Julie and me. She gave me a little air kiss. "You, too, E.C. What a *coinkydink*" (that crowd's slang for "coincidence") "that you two hang out together and you won first and second."

"We bribed the judges," I said.

"Well, we know *Julie* would have enough to bribe them, anyway."

I think she would have liked to believe it. It's hard to lose. It doesn't help the view from Tryvannshogda.

There was an accordion player ruining "White Christmas" next, followed by Coach McCarthy reading the new year's basketball schedule—dates and places.

We closed with the singing of three Christmas carols.

When assembly was over, a lot of kids called out their congratulations to Julie and me.

Some of the younger ones lined up in the hall for Julie's autograph on copies of her essay.

She kept saying over and over that she couldn't believe it, and her eyes were dancing and crying at the same time.

We walked down the hall together, and she asked me if I wanted to come back to Peligro with her. The Hummer was outside.

"I have to go with Mom while we get our tree," I said.

"Oh, Eddie, what a day for me!"

"Yeah. What a day!"

"For you too. Congratulations to you too."

"Thanks."

Then she stopped in her tracks and turned to me. "Listen, Eddie. Do you think I should ask The Sluts for Peale's birthday? I think they'd really like me if they got to know me."

I wanted to say *I* think they'd make mincemeat of you. They aren't well-wishers. They aren't friendly. Feed them at your own risk.

I said, "I think people already have plans for Christmas Eve."

We stopped by our lockers for our coats, then headed out the front door, where the Hummer waited in the line of parents' cars.

"Julie? Julie, wait!" Patsy Persea came hurrying up to us, carrying something gift wrapped. "Here's a present, Julie."

"For *me*?"

"The winner gets beaucoup gifts! We decided to make it a tradition!"

Then came Meredith Merola, Kay Hicks, Clio Hamilton, and Raleigh Raines—all Sluts, all bringing presents to Julie.

They were calling out their congratulations and wishing her a merry Christmas.

I was hanging back, watching, thinking I was wrong about them making mincemeat of Julie. I wished her aunt could see it.

"Thanks! Oh, thank you!" Julie was exclaiming. She couldn't stop the tears any longer. They were running down her face past the lenses of her Guccis. Her nose was red. She was giggling, and she told me, "I'm hideously embarrassed, Eddie. I don't have anything for any of them!"

"You weren't supposed to. They didn't win anything." I took some of the packages and carried her prize for her, the huge gold pen with her name on it.

Julie said, "Well, Eddie? Are you going to admit you were wrong about them?" Then she laughed and said, "You don't have to. I don't care. I'm so happy."

We had reached the Hummer, with Peale up front beside Mrs. Slaymaster.

Even though it was dark by then, and the cars waiting had their lights on, the streetlight above us helped me see what The Sluts had given Julie. A few days before I'd helped wrap them: some in red paper with white trees, some in white paper with red trees. They were the Christmas-wrapped empty boxes from under the school tree.

Julie opened the front door and we put the boxes inside.

"What on earth are those?" Mrs. S. grumbled.

"Presents from friends." Julie slammed the front door while I opened the back door for her. She crawled inside, taking the enormous pen from my hands, saying, "Don't say I don't have friends, Aunt Rosalind, and don't say I'm not a writer."

"I never said you weren't a writer; I said you don't have anything to write about."

Julie didn't need me there for one of Mrs. Slaymaster's *I told you so*'s. It's bad enough to be humiliated; it's worse to have one of your friends see it.

"I'm late," I said. "I can't wait!"

Julie said, "You're jelly, aren't you, Eddie?" She was reaching out for one of the packages wrapped in red paper with white trees. She continued in Slutspeak: "If you don't get in this car this minute, I'll know what a jelly belly you really are, Eddie Tobbit!"

"Tobbit?" Mrs. S. shouted. "The door's open! Get in!"

I couldn't. I wasn't just sparing Julie's feelings. I was also sparing myself the pain of seeing the look on her face when she realized what The Sluts had done.

I slammed the door of the Hummer and took off.

Seven

Christmas Eve, the night of the party, a smiling young man opened the door for my mother, Darwin C. Duke, and me. Then, miraculously, he was waiting in the cloakroom to take our coats, his face creased with an angry scowl, a pencil-thin mustache above his lip.

"I knew I shouldn't have made us those martinis," my mother said to the doctor. "I'm seeing double."

"You're seeing twins," Doctor Duke said.

That was our first real meeting with Diego and Paulo Parla.

They were about five nine with great hair, as silky as it was thick and straight. They made me feel like something the cat dragged in, both of them in black dinner jackets, white shirts, and black bow ties.

I was wearing a pair of brown corduroy Dockers and a

tan mock turtleneck sweater, and my mother hadn't really dressed up much either. She was in her tweed suit, with a sweater and low heels, because she'd felt foolish last time when Mrs. S. wore jeans.

Although Mom and I looked like gate crashers, the doctor was the Pillsbury Doughboy dressed by Calvin Klein.

Short and pudgy, he had lost all the hair at the front of his head, although he had quite a crop of wiry gray hair in the rear. This he kept long and tied back in a ponytail, with a red silk scarf.

He wore a navy blazer with gold buttons, a white shirt with a navy knit tie, navy trousers, and oxblood ankle boots. A red handkerchief matching the one guarding his ponytail peeked from his top pocket. Into his lapel he'd tucked a white rose he must have plucked from the small bouquet of white roses he'd bought my mother for her birthday. There were five left. My twelve red ones made his bouquet look chintzy.

Even before we got into the living room, I could sense that what would be waiting in there for us would not be other guests dressed for a night at the movies. I could hear music and a certain bustle.

"You said this wasn't going to be anything fancy," my mother complained to me.

"No, *you* said is it going to be fancy and *I* said I doubt it."

"It isn't really fancy, Ann," The Duck said, as though he

had seen fancy and nothing waiting for us in the rooms ahead would be it. "You look very attractive. Relax, my darling."

His darling? I flinched.

"My name is Paulo," said the glowering twin who'd taken our coats. "Go right in."

"I'm E.C. Tobbit, this is my mother, Ann Tobbit, and this is Doctor Duke."

We began the long walk down the marble hall toward the living room.

"E.C., it isn't customary to introduce oneself and party to the servants," said Doctor Duke.

I shrugged, trying to react to my supposed gaffe low-key. "He started it." My face was red. I could feel it.

My mother said, "I *wish* I'd known it was a formal party."

"It's not a truly formal party," said The World's Foremost Authority On Social Customs. "That would mean black tie."

Then we saw Mrs. S.

She was waiting to welcome us. There was a string quartet behind her, and maybe two dozen guests nibbling off silver trays passed by uniformed maids.

I recognized some of the faces, most of them owners of real estate or insurance companies in Serenity, the BMW dealer, the types who went to Rotary Tuesdays at The Canal House.

The aroma of fresh flowers filled the air, and the room seemed lighted only by candles, all sizes and shapes, everywhere.

But it was Mrs. S. who captured my attention.

She looked as though she had come straight from one of those makeovers afternoon talk shows sometimes have. She was definitely not the same person I'd last seen behind the wheel of the Hummer.

Her silver hair was curled, and there were small diamond clips nestled in it. Head to high heels she was in red velvet, with more tiny diamonds glittering around her neck and on a bracelet. There was a diamond ring the size of an Excedrin tablet weighing down the third finger of her left hand.

"Merry Christmas, Ann and E.C.," she called. "And *you* must be—"

"Dr. Darwin Duke, psychotherapist," he boomed forth, always naming his profession so no one would mistake him for a dentist.

Mrs. S. shook all of our hands. Then she said, "And happy birthday, Ann!"

"Oh, thank you for remembering."

I liked Mrs. S. for that.

"Let me introduce you to everyone, Ann and Doctor Duke . . . E.C., the young people are in the solarium. Go down the hall and take the first door on your right."

"I have a friend who'll be arriving soon," I said.

"Not who I think it is?" Doctor Duke had lowered his voice to ask the question.

He knew Neal was my only friend, as well as I knew the doctor did not like socializing with clients.

"We'll stay clear of you," I said.

"Oh, *never mind*," my mother whispered to him.

"Just ignore us," I said.

Mrs. Slaymaster said to go and tell Diego, at the door, and he would direct my friend to the solarium.

"Mrs. Slaymaster, how do you tell those twins apart?" My mother wanted to get off the subject upsetting Quack Quack.

"Diego's the sun," she replied. "Paulo's the night.'

"*What* an insightful remark!" from Guess Who.

Eight

Julie was sometimes unexpectedly pretty. She was that night. She had on one of those ankle-length black silk dresses that look like a long slip, spaghetti straps holding it up. Somehow she had managed to tame the Brillo, tying it with a thin black ribbon, and the only piece of jewelry she wore was the thinnest gold bracelet.

She said, "Thanks, pal. I wondered why you wouldn't stay while I opened just one package."

"I wish I could have warned you somehow, or stopped it. It happened so fast."

"I wanted to call you, but Aunt grounded all activity for twenty-four hours, plus I owe her a week at Lucky Star. . . . That's how she traps me into going there with her. She builds it into my punishment."

"Punishment for what?"

"Aunt doesn't like me broadcasting family business. She says my essay about Mama was washing dirty linen in public."

Most of the kids in the solarium were sons and daughters of local contractors and plumbers. But there were also kids from Chalfont and other preppies whose dads or moms were local lawyers, doctors, realtors, and restaurant owners. Some of them were wearing buttons opposing the name Sonny Fitch Park.

"I know why you look different tonight," I said to Julie. "The Guccis are gone."

"I've got my contacts in."

We found a corner of the solarium near a lighted five-foot angel where we could talk. I told her about Neal, his thing for Stephen King, and his far-out clothes.

She said she didn't know any of the kids there, and thank heaven she hadn't asked The Sluts.

The solarium was so dark and crowded, it was hard to see furnishings. Besides long leather couches with low tables in front of them, there seemed to be nothing but fish tanks. They lined the walls. They were filled with green branches, small golden castles, and tiny white stones that sparkled in the light, and swimming through it all these small blue-and-brown fish, hundreds of them.

There was a tape playing, and I caught a little of Jonatha Brooks singing "Amelia."

Julie said, "I bet you don't know the poem that inspired that song."

"I don't read a lot of poetry." That was like saying I didn't use bath salts a lot. Half the time I didn't get poetry. I got Charles Bukowski, but not many others. I didn't get the poems of my father's favorite poet, Wallace Stevens, any of the time.

Julie said, "The poem is by Sharon Olds. It's called 'I Go Back to May 1937.' She imagines that she's watching her parents get ready to marry. She thinks of trying to stop them, warn them of all the awful things they're going to do to each other and their children. . . . But she doesn't, because she wants to be born and live her life. . . . That's neat, isn't it? I can't get it out of my head," she said.

"I wonder if Neal will find us okay." I was looking around for him.

"You didn't even hear what I said, did you, E.C.?"

"I sort of did—a poem by a woman inspired the song."

"Never mind," Julie said. "I put someone who'll listen to me way up there on my wish list, along with Aunt one day leaving Texas forever. . . . Don't worry about your friend. Diego will take his name and Paulo will help him find his way here."

"The sun and the night, according to your aunt."

"I know she says that. *I* say that at last Dr. Jekyll and Mr. Hyde are two people!"

"Which one's Mr. Hyde?"

"Paulo," said Julie. "The one with the little thin mustache who never smiles. Diego's all teeth, jokes, just the opposite."

"Did they come from Texas with you?"

"Yes, they're always with us. Mr. and Mrs. Parla and their sons. Aunt likes to say they're part of the family, but she doesn't even pay them scale, and she sticks them down in the caretaker's cottage."

We sat in the solarium until it became so noisy we couldn't talk. There were Dutchman Park balloons and banners beginning to appear. Some of the kids were pasting stickers on the furniture and across the fronts of the aquariums: *Sonny Fitch—what a bitch!*

"I hate that Aunt's making them change the name of the park," Julie said.

"Did you ever meet Sonny Fitch?"

"Oh, no. I came into Aunt's life much later."

"Neal says that the only way the Dutchman Park diehards will ever get anywhere is to play down-and-dirty like she does."

"It sounds like Neal has delusions of grandeur. Aunt outsmarts everybody. Doesn't he know that by now?"

"Neal has his diabolic side too."

"You really like him, don't you? I hope I will."

"You will. Just remember something: He dresses up in weird clothes."

"Like what?"

"You never know like what. I'm just warning you."

"Maybe he's upstairs with the adults. Let's have a look."

She started moving rapidly through the crowd. "Don't you hate the fact that we only have a few more years before we're adults?"

"I never think about it. Why do you?"

"Because I can't imagine what will become of me. Aunt says it's something you *can't* imagine." She grabbed my hand and began pulling me along with her. "Aunt says no matter what you see for yourself in the future, you'll always be way off the mark."

Nine

On the mantel in the living room stood the gold pen Julie had won.

"Aunt isn't happy about its being there," she said. "She thinks it's ugly, and she says why should I get an award for announcing that I came from bad blood?"

Peale was standing there on a chair by the mantel, his head turned up as though he could not take his twinkling green glass eyes away from the gold pen.

He was dressed in a white dinner jacket, black tie, black pumps like a girl's, patent leather with bows on them. He had a red rosebud in his lapel.

A familiar deep voice said, "I hear *you* won something, too."

"Yes, ma'am, Mrs. Slaymaster. I got second prize." I was

hoping she wouldn't ask me what my essay was about, and she didn't.

"I hope *you* weren't wallowing in family mud!" she said, a pleasant smile masking her sour message. She looked as though she was telling me the names of birds that visited Peligro's feeders in winter. "Julie, here, can't seem to find the doughnut, only the hole." *Wrens, nuthatches, cardinals and their wives, smile smile.*

"I see the doughnut, Aunt. I see you very clearly."

"What you don't do is *hear* me. I thought I told you to get that thing down off the mantel before the party started." *Downy woodpeckers and tufted titmice.*

I made a stab at defending Julie, saying, "I wish *I'd* won that pen!"

"I bet you *do*," Mrs. S. said sarcastically, as though I'd said I wish I'd won the prize for scarfing down the most wieners at the 4-H Livestock Show. But she was smiling graciously from ear to ear.

Then she placed her hands on Julie's shoulders and turned her around. "Go tell Diego to check the punch in the solarium. He's to see if anyone's spiked it, and remove it if someone has. This is the time of night those preppies get out their flasks. Hurry, Julie."

When Julie left, Mrs. Slaymaster turned back to me. "You knew those boxes were empty! I saw the look on your face. That's why you beat it!"

I could feel my neck get hot. I knew I'd turned beet red. The body is no great friend when the going gets tough.

I said, "I didn't think Julie wanted me to see her be humiliated."

"Why? What's so special about *you*?"

How do you answer that one?

I didn't. I just stood there. The string quartet was playing Paul McCartney's "Maybe I'm Amazed." Some people were dancing out in the foyer. More were sitting around the living room balancing china plates on their knees, eating ham and escalloped potatoes. The uniformed maids with white S's embroidered on the aprons of their black uniforms were offering everyone champagne.

Mrs. Slaymaster said, "I'm going home next week. I hope you'll keep an eye on Julie. I don't want to have to be running back and forth for every little crisis. . . . I'm not saying be her bodyguard or anything major. Just be her friend."

"I already am."

"Try being her friend so it *shows*," she said.

Without skipping a beat, while my face still smarted from that remark, she squished up her features as though she was going to cry and said, "Oh boo hoo boo hoo. They wrapped empty boxes, boo hoo, and pretended they were Christmas presents, sob!"

I didn't know what she was up to.

She said, "Is that a big deal to you?"

"I thought it was pretty crappy."

"It was pretty crappy, but that's all it was. Pretty crappy. Not worth bawling your eyes out over. She's got an IQ as high as a cat's back, but all she cares about is being liked. That's too bad, because she's too eager. Those Sluts, those high and mighty little bitches, smell need the same as sharks smell blood, and they go in for the kill."

I was thinking of Ro Ro Fitch running down Front Street with her bra and blouse up in the trees.

"She's never had it hard, either," Mrs. Slaymaster said.

"Isn't it hard when your mother dies and you're only four and you don't have a father?" I said.

"My mother died in childbirth. My father was illiterate. His whole life he was known to everyone just as Sonny. Like some street dog."

She wasn't a person you wanted to compete with for My Childhood Was Worse Than Anyone's.

"I had no Auntie to take me in," she went on, "no one to take me to live on a six-hundred-fifty-acre ranch, with my own pony, and so many toys in my bedroom I can't count them. Oh, what a hard life!"

"Well," I began, and she knew I didn't have a finish, didn't even wait to see if it was possible.

She said, "Julie should wait until she's got something to write about! You probably should, too!"

I fished around my mind for how this conversation had

58

started, and then I said, "I'll be happy to look out for Julie, if that's what this is about, ma'am."

She put out her hand.

"Deal!" she said.

I said, "Deal!" back.

I was surprised that her handshake was on the limp side, when I'd braced myself for something more like a vise.

"Your mother's birthday cake was brought to her in here and cut, then sent down to the solarium. You just missed it."

I wanted to say something about appreciating that she did that for Mom, but my mind's eye suddenly landed on the hall table back at our house, where I'd put Peale's astrology chart so I wouldn't forget it. I'd told Mom that was one less worry she had: I'd take charge of seeing that it went to Peligro with us.

I'd forgotten all about it.

I was about to explain that to Mrs. Slaymaster, but when I looked, she was gone. Coming toward me, grinning, was Neal as I'd never seen him before. There was nothing quirky about his clothes. A dark suit, white shirt, rep tie. He wasn't wearing the small gold earring, and his hair was combed back neatly. He looked as he did when he was partnering someone in the KDS dance recitals, real vanilla.

"You just missed meeting Mrs. Slaymaster," I told him.

"I'll live."

I said, "When did you decide to look normal?"

"That's my disguise tonight, Easy."

Ten

Neal reached inside his jacket and brought out a small, gift-wrapped package, which he handed to Julie.

"It's not a Christmas present," Neal said. "It's just me saying thanks for having me."

"Thanks for coming," Julie said.

"I almost didn't get here. My car broke down. My mother had to bring me."

"You can ride home with us," I said.

"No, she'll pick me up. What an extravaganza! Wow!" Neal grinned down at Julie. I liked it that he didn't try to hide how impressed he was by Peligro. I went the other way. As we'd come from the solarium, Julie had shown me Cinema S. It held forty leather seats and smelled like the inside of a rich man's car. When I'd asked her what all the light-brown shawls with the S on them were for, Julie'd said they were cashmere screening-room throws. In my best blasé voice I'd said, "That's what I thought."

Neal continued to rave. "I love your aquarium! All kilifish, my father's favorite."

Julie was looking up at him, laughing, admiring him. Yes, Neal was her cup of tea, I thought.

"I'm going to save this and open it later," Julie said, putting the gift Neal'd brought her up on a ledge of the bookshelf. "Thanks."

I decided to let them enjoy each other.

Way down at the end of the living room, in an alcove, I could see Charlie Bannon, the old curmudgeon who was our lawyer and used to be my Cub Scout leader back in the years when I was learning to make a lanyard and do the scissors kick.

Charlie was standing by the tall doors leading to the wraparound porch. One of the doors was open a crack. Charlie and a few others standing there were still in Marlboro Country.

"Merry Christmas, Mr. Bannon."

"Same to you, E.C. Your old man's probably rolling over in his grave seeing you up here on the hill."

"You think I'd be here if I thought he could see me?"

When Evans Above was first being turned into Peligro, the rumors were that Mrs. Slaymaster was bringing illegals up from Texas in her Hummer so she wouldn't have to pay locals the going rate.

61

My father had done an editorial for *The Banner*, one of his few opinion pieces, describing landmark edifices built by slave labor: the pyramids, the Roman Colosseum, etc.

He had not mentioned Mrs. S. or the house she was reconstructing, but everyone knew what Dad meant.

Charlie lit a new Camel from a spent one.

I said, "Even if this wasn't taking place at Peligro, Dad would have hated this party, sir. He never liked big parties where you couldn't hear the music."

"Frank didn't need to hear the music. He was like me—he wasn't a dancer. I remember your mother'd try to get him out on the floor. He'd rather walk into scalding water."

He let a half inch of ash drop from his Camel to the rug.

I reached for one of the round silver ashtrays with S monogrammed on it.

"That was Rose's niece you were just with, wasn't it, E.C.?"

"Yes. Her name's Julie."

"Julie Calldownthemoon Slaymaster, thanks to Peale. Did you hear that one? That she adopted Julie to keep Peale company? She told me that once. She believes Peale guides her and brings her luck."

"That's why my mother gets along with her," I said. "They aren't slaves to logic."

Charlie let out one of those wheezy laughs lifetime smokers often have. "Peale gets the credit for everything. I saw Simon

Slaymaster just after he got Peale. I think his mind was going along with his liver. Peale was supposed to be a Christmas present for Rose. But he had the damn doll at the ranch for weeks before. And *that* was when he finally made this Full-flusher of his work. Simon found a way to get oil out of the ground faster. Or if you wanted to believe a jolly old fat man who was about to meet his maker, *Peale* found the way."

"You're not superstitious, Mr. Bannon?"

"Peale is a chunk of animal hide. Simon Slaymaster was a genius. He had only one flaw. He was married to Serenity's own Queen of Greed."

A sardonic laugh from Charlie, which turned into a fit of coughing.

Then he said, "And it's a sad story, E.C. She got her revenge on this hometown of hers. She's the chief landlord. But she's never enjoyed the benefits, doesn't know how to. I was down in Texas once and she was pricing some cattle, complaining to me the figure was too high, so I teased her. I said, 'By now you ought not to be afraid of being poor any-more, Rose.' This was a little after Simon's death. I'd gone to The Lucky Star on my usual mission, to see if I could get her to stop raising the rents up here so high. She said, 'Char-lie, I'm not afraid of being poor. I'm afraid of not being rich.'"

"She never acts rich, though."

"I just told you!" said the Cubmaster. *Dear God in a*

bucket, Cub Scout Tobbit, don't you know how to secure a hawser to a bitt? She doesn't enjoy her money. She *counts* it!"

I stayed talking with him awhile longer, mostly about how he never understood Simon's choosing Rose to marry, except that Simon's sister had been homely as a hedge fence as well.

"Men often marry their sisters or their mothers," said Charlie. "You'd be doing yourself a favor if you could marry your mother."

"Thanks. I'll tell her that."

When I turned around, I saw my mother dancing with Dr. Duke on the hardwood floor down at the end of the living room, and off to one side in the alcove, Neal was dancing with Julie. As usual when Neal danced, he made his partner look good, not as good as he was, but probably better than she was. And as usual, a few people stopped what they were doing and watched.

After the last dance was announced, I cut in.

"You two are good together," I told Julie.

"*He's* why."

It was near midnight when the quartet put down their instruments.

Soon after, a violin began playing softly in the background. Paulo appeared with his regal, disgruntled bearing, and sounded an enormous golden gong. The ubiquitous S shone in its center.

Everyone stopped talking.

Mrs. Slaymaster, in her long red gown, swooped Peale up and walked into the large foyer with him. Her guests all followed.

I found myself walking with Julie.

"What's happening?"

"You'll see," she said.

The violinist started playing again. Mrs. Slaymaster, with Peale in her arms, began to waltz in circles across the gleaming white marble floor.

A voice began to trill, *"Feel-ings . . ."*

It was a very high voice, the sort you sometimes hear piping out from a church choir.

". . . noth-ing more than feel-ings . . ." It took me several seconds to realize it was Rosalind Slaymaster herself singing, her normally deep, gruff voice raised several octaves as she whirled in circles holding Peale close.

Beside me, Julie whispered, "That was her song with Mr. Slaymaster. Now it's her song with Peale."

Just then Neal's mother arrived. She stood on the sidelines, a black velvet cape over her shoulders, a floppy black hat arranged over one eye, a grim look on her face. KDS, her dance studio, was housed in a building owned by Rosalind Slaymaster. Mrs. Slaymaster had owned the building Kraft Drugs was located in, too. Neal would get furious when his mother would blame his father's suicide on the final rent raise that drove him out of business. He'd say, You don't kill yourself over a damn rent raise! Just wait, Mrs. Kraft would answer. Just wait until you're his age and whatever it is you're doing is done and over.

I could see Neal back in the alcove, unaware she was there. He was holding a silver cigarette lighter for Charlie. In the other hand he was holding a bidi between his thumb and forefinger, the tough-guy way he always smoked a cigarette.

His eyebrows rose when our eyes met, and he grinned, as if he was saying, Oh, wow, E.C., is this not way cool?

When Mrs. S. sang toward the end: "*You'll nev-er come a-gain,*" a new, strong baritone voice joined in.

I looked in its direction and saw the short, portly figure, little arms raised so that a gold cufflink brushed against the gold buttons on the blue blazer.

"*Wo-o-o, feel-ings.*" Doctor Duke had stopped her for a beat.

Then, an amazed tilt gracing Mrs. S's eyebrows, they both warbled, ". . . *feel you a-gain in my arms.*"

The guests began applauding and exclaiming. I looked back, ready to make a face at Neal, who was holding the silver lighter one minute, then the next sliding it inside his jacket.

Eleven

The doctor had a green Saab convertible with HEADOC on the license plate.

The moment we started down the long, winding hill after the party, Mom said, "I had no idea you liked to sing that much, Darwin." (I translated that as: *How* could you *humiliate* us by joining in a song that was obviously her special one!)

"You know that I sing in St. Luke's choir. Solos. You know that, Ann."

"Did Mrs. Slaymaster say anything to you about it?"

"I have a hunch Rosalind quite enjoyed it." He glanced across at Mom and said, "But *you* forgot the horoscope for Peale, didn't you?"

That was the good doctor, for you: Rub it in!

I said, "*I* forgot it!"

"I'll take it there tomorrow," Mom said.

"And what . . . on *earth* . . . was Shirley Kraft doing there tonight? How in heaven's name did *she* get into the picture?" asked Dr. D.

"I thought Shirley looked very glamorous," my mother said. "She reminded me of the old days, when people said she looked just like Debbie Reynolds and Perry Kraft looked like Van Cliburn."

"How she looked is beside the point, Ann!"

I said, "I thought she looked good, too." Dog pile on the rabbit!

"The point is *not* how she got herself up! The point is that she should not be somewhere she is not welcome!"

"Why do we have to go into this on Christmas Eve?" Mom said.

The doctor sighed as though the weight of the world rested on his exhausted shoulders. "Because I happen to like Rosalind," he announced. "I happen to feel protective toward her."

"She isn't in any danger from Shirley Kraft," said my mother.

"Don't be too sure!" Then he wagged a finger in the air. "And how dare those Dutchman roughnecks rub her nose in their opinions?"

"Darwin, you're making mountains out of molehills," Mom told him.

"Mrs. Kraft was there only at the end, to pick up Neal," I said.

"She didn't even take her cape off," said my mother.

"Lucky for us," said the doctor. "It would have reflected back on us, since E.C. was the one who asked Neal. Shirley Kraft is almost pathological on the subject of Rosalind, as I'm sure E.C. might well know . . . as well as he knows my disinclination to socialize with clients."

I felt like saying: You don't know the half of it, Darwin, old boy. While you were exercising your vocal cords, your client was exercising his fingers.

"Let's not spoil things by quibbling," my mother pleaded. "It's been such a lovely Christmas Eve."

"Neal didn't bother you, did he, Doctor?" I couldn't let go yet. "I didn't see him anywhere near you."

"We were in the *same room* together, in a *social* situation," Doctor Duke hissed.

"So what? It wasn't more than an hour! Neal and his mother left right after your little duet with Mrs. Slaymaster!"

My mother shoved in one of his tapes, Sinatra singing. Sinatra always sang in his car, and in his waiting room. He'd already announced that the last song to play at his funeral was to be Frankie singing "Hey, Look, No Crying." (How about any laughing?)

"My Way" filled the car. Darwin Duke knew all the words. I imagined him riding around singing about how he chewed up his mistakes and spit them out.

When we got to our house, I left them in the Saab. I could tell they were on the verge of what my mother liked to call "a disagreement." It was going to be big and noisy—that much I knew, because what he'd said about Neal's mother was the kind of petty dog do that raised the hackles on my mother's back.

Selfishly, I was thinking this could be the end, for once and for all, of The Duck in my life. Finally, she had to see what a little creep he was. My mother was timid enough at social gatherings. She didn't need to be escorted by a pony-tailed fatso with two red silk hankies who fancied himself The Life of the Party.

I ran inside.

I couldn't wait to get to the computer and see Julie's take on the party.

Doon had his leash in his mouth, and he was dancing around signaling he was ready for his walk.

Arbus, the Siamese, knew me like a book—knew what I was going to do before I did it.

She was stretched out across the IBM keyboard, no doubt torn between keeping her eyes shut as though she was fast asleep and keeping one open so she'd see me go ape.

The open eye won out.

"Arbus! Get down! GET . . . DOWN!"

She finally picked herself up and sashayed down to the end of the table, tail swishing disdainfully.

"Give me just a minute, Doon," I begged.

He begged back, sitting up with his leash still in his mouth.

I went into the IBM anyway, where I knew there'd be mail from Jslay.

I totally like Neal, Eddie. I didn't see anything weird about the way he dressed.

Aunt's going to the ranch New Year's Eve. I wish we could watch the fireworks from here, but she doesn't let me entertain boys nights when she's out of town. So we want to go to Ellie Cloward's party. Neal has to be late. Can you escort me there?

Well, good night. Wo-o-o, feelings! J.

P.S. Neal gave me the nicest gift. Stephen King's "Skeleton Crew."

Twelve

I called Neal the next morning. "I thought you only stole from corporations like the Bookworm or the A&P?"

"What are you talking about?"

"A silver lighter with an S on it."

"Man, I'm not even awake yet and you're on my case!"

I said, "I get you in up there, and you swipe the silver!"

"She won't even know it's gone."

"That's not the point! You could have gotten me eighty-sixed from Peligro. You could have gotten Julie in trouble, too."

"If you're going to have a psychotic episode over a little souvenir I took, I'll return it. I'll give it to you, and you can sneak it back. Okay?"

"I'd just like to hear an apology."

"I'm sorry. Okay? And hey, Merry Christmas."

"Do you get it at all, Neal? Your stealing sucks!"

"I *heard* you, E.C.! . . . Now you hear me. Guess what's playing in Lamberton? Think prom dress. Think blood."

"Think Sissy Spacek," I said.

"Right. Think Sissy Spacek playing the ultimate victim, Carietta White."

I could almost see her in this long dress, on some guy's arm, smiling like a million-dollar lottery winner, a second before the bucket of pig's blood came down on her head. Stephen King knew how to hurt a girl.

"We can't miss *Carrie*, E.C. I've got a tango lesson to give tomorrow at noon, but then Julie and I are going to the movies. Want to come?"

"You said you just woke up. When did you decide this?"

"Last night." Then, quickly, he added, "She doesn't know anything about my souvenir, does she?"

"I didn't tell her."

"I think *Carrie* is the best movie Sissy Spacek ever made, E.C. Would you agree?"

"I liked her best in *Badlands*," I said.

"Oh, with Martin Sheen. Yeah. I'd forgotten that evil flick!"

"Maybe Julie'd rather be alone with you."

"We want you with us. Besides, we've got Auntie to worry about. I don't care to meet Auntie. She wouldn't like a Kraft taking her niece out, and I don't want to give her the satisfaction of telling me I can't."

"So you want me to pick up Julie?"

"Would you, Easy?" His affectionate name for me, times he wanted something, I thought. But that wasn't really fair to Neal. *He* was the easy one, the one always trying to rise above it. Read something, wear something, have a theory about something to get you past life's fastballs. About the only thing that rattled him was any explanation about why his father hanged himself. Neal liked to say maybe he was just a melancholy soul, the kind that marches to a different drummer.

Neal's outfit was toned down, for Neal. He had a Russian armored unit officer's cap on his head, complete with a red-and-gold hammer-and-sickle symbol, and his standard navy pea jacket had a British desert rat unit patch. But otherwise he wore jeans, a red sweater, old Nikes.

He was in this expansive mood, taking his time at the candy counter to get just the right things, changing our seats while we waited for the movie, and talking a mile a minute about whether he should go to Penn State or take a job on a cruise ship and see the world.

When Julie asked him what he wanted to study, he said he had a theory that you should never commit yourself that much to the future until you'd tried different subjects, all sorts of directions, and maybe even traveled for years before going to college.

"What you're going to be someday is a lot like who you're going to be it with. Both take lots of trial and error and thought, Jewel, and if you make a mistake in either area, you could be doomed."

Julie was looking up at him adoringly, nodding in agreement, saying "Right!" and "Yes!" and "I know!"

Jewel and Easy, I thought, and I was slightly uncomfortable all through the movie. I knew he had ahold of her hand, and his arm was around the back of her seat. But he was quiet once the movie started. Neal was always quiet at a Stephen King movie.

After, Neal had to get right back. He had a lesson at five thirty and one at six. We didn't even stop at the drive-in for Cokes but zipped into Serenity, Neal playing Brian McKnight's "Never Felt This Way." I sat in back so they could have the whole front seat, but Julie sat as close to Neal as she would have if I hadn't.

Thirteen

New Year's Eve afternoon I got Mom to take a break and let me treat her to lunch.

That was when she told me that Aunt Sheila and The Duck were coming for dinner. They were both staying overnight because champagne was being served. Mom didn't want either of them on the roads after drinking.

"Who's sleeping where?"

"Sheila will be in with me, and Darwin will be on the living-room couch. I almost broke the date after last night."

"What happened, or is it too gross to tell me?"

Mom laughed. "No, it's not gross. We just don't always have the same take on life. We had an argument about the chicken poem—that's what I call it. A client brought it in to Darwin, and Darwin showed it to me, saying the client thought it was optimistic, when it was just the opposite. I

thought it was optimistic too. So we had one of our dis-
agreements."

"I'd like to see the poem."

"I made a copy for you," she said. "When we go back to
the shop, I'll give it to you. Show it to Neal and Julie. See
what they think. And don't tell them ahead of time what
Darwin had to say about it."

"Okay."

Then she said, "Something else, honey. Darwin and I
are going to Saint Martin for a week in February."

"How can you stand him for a week?"

"You see him in a whole other light, E.C. I see him as
good company and as a good dancer. You know how I love
to dance."

I remembered Charlie Bannon remarking on how my
mother'd try to get Dad out on the floor.

"And he helped you, honey," Mom said. "Remember
that. You didn't have a bad word to say about him until we
started dating."

"He's just a long way from what Dad was," I said.

"Who isn't?"

"Just because he can *dance*."

"Hush."

Then Mom said, "What about you and Julie? You've
been spending a lot of time up there."

"You know what's neat? Mrs. S. has a place called The

Dome, built on top of the house. She has a mini observatory there. You can see into all the windows in Serenity!"

"Then I'm not worried about you," Mom said.

"What do you mean?"

"I mean if you and Julie are busy looking in other people's windows, you're not all that wrapped up in each other."

"We're friends," I said.

"Just checking," said Mom.

Julie was so terrified that something would go wrong and Mrs. Slaymaster would have to change her traveling plans for New Year's, she didn't see Neal after our movie date. She said she didn't want her aunt to think anything important was going on in her life. I said it was a good thing I had a rugged ego, or I'd take it as an insult that for the past few days she'd asked me by for movies under the cashmere robes in Cinema S, and Scrabble games in the solarium. Rosalind Slaymaster would poke her nose in the door at some point and say, "Hello, Tobbit," in that way she had of making my name sound like "two bit."

"She doesn't see you as threatening at all," Julie said, "but she would Neal. He's older and he's flashier. Plus Neal says not to even tell her his last name, because there's a grudge going way back, between Aunt and the Krafts."

"She's got a grudge against this whole town, not just the Krafts."

"Isn't it silly?" Julie said. "I'd never hold anything

against anyone for years and years and years. Would you, Eddie?"

"I hope not."

Mom agreed to pick Julie up that night and drive us to the Clowards'. I just couldn't tell her that Julie wasn't really my date—she was Neal's. I knew Mom wouldn't have liked the chicanery.

Mrs. Slaymaster came out to the car long enough to compliment my mother on Peale's horoscope. Then she gave Julie's arm a punch, which I guessed was in place of a good-bye kiss. Mrs. S. was on her way to Texas in a few hours.

I got out of the front seat and into the back with Julie, and we started down the winding hill.

"How long will Mrs. Slaymaster be gone?" my mother asked.

"A month or two."

"And Mrs. Parla takes care of you?"

"No, she's the cook and general housekeeper. The Parlas live down in the caretaker's cottage. But Mrs. Rosenkrantz stays with me when Aunt goes. And Bob, her dachshund."

Then, "Guess what!" Julie whispered to me.

"What?"

"I told Mrs. Rosenkrantz she could leave after Aunt does. I gave her the night off. She's going to her sister's."

Mom could hear us talking softly, so she shoved in a

tape. Phil Collins. At least it wasn't Ol' Blue Eyes.

"So?"

"So we *can* go to Peligro! We can watch the fireworks from The Dome."

"If Neal comes for us in time."

"He will. This is his idea. He didn't want me to tell you."

"Why?'

"He was afraid you wouldn't want to disobey Aunt's orders."

"Neal thought *I'd* put up an argument?"

Julie nodded. "He says you don't like to break rules. . . . I wasn't sure I could figure out how to do it without Aunt knowing. A lot depended on whether or not the housekeeper would take the night off, knowing she had to keep it a secret from Aunt. . . . I finally got it all together this morning."

"I hope he knows all the trouble you went through."

"It's not trouble when it's what you want too."

"I think I should stay at the Clowards' party."

"That would ruin everything, Eddie!"

"How can it ruin everything? Don't you two want to be alone?"

"You're part of us, E.C.!" Julie said.

"But are you falling for Neal?"

"Not yet." She giggled. "I'm going to wait and seeski."

Slutspeak reared its ugly head. I groaned.

Neal showed up at the Clowards' party just as Julie and
I were ready to give up on him.

He was wearing an old, moth-eaten uniform, probably
something a high school drum major had worn. Black pants
with red stripes. A light-blue jacket with gold-braid epaulets
and brass buttons. His black officer's cap, with light-blue
piping and a gold cord, was tipped over one eye.

He swept Julie out onto the living-room floor after telling
me to get our coats, that his car was outside with the motor
running.

It was snowing just a little, one of those odd times when
the moon and stars show in the same sky with snow.

"Can we put the top down, Neal?" Julie asked.

"Sure. Ruin the car," I said.

"There's no way to ruin this baby." It was a '93 Chevy
Cavalier. Neal reached up and unhooked the latches.

Behind me the top landed in its berth with a thump.

"Where were you this time last year, Julie?" Neal said.

"At this huge party on the ranch with mariachi music
and piñatas. Aunt asked everyone who worked for us to
come, and everyone did except for Paulo, Diego, and all the
others anywhere near my age. They had their own party
somewhere."

I felt like that was what I'd do the rest of that night: have my own party somewhere in my head. I put my coat collar up and leaned back, looking up at the stars.

Neal said, "I have a theory about New Year's Eve. And we have only an hour and a half to go."

"Uh-oh, another theory." Julie said it as though she knew Neal all too well, instead of for about a week.

"You set yourself on New Year's Eve, the same as you might set a clock. You run according to how you were set. I believe that what you do on New Year's Eve starts you down the path of what you'll do all year."

"With the same people?" Julie asked.

"Or people like them," Neal said.

"Is that why you said we should be at Peligro?"

"That's why," Neal said. "Let's all go for a swim in the pool; then I'll make everybody breakfast."

All the while we drove toward Peligro, Julie watched him.

He must have felt her eyes on him.

Fourteen

The first thing we saw when we got inside Peligro was this enormous orchid tree. It was positioned awkwardly in the hall where Mrs. Slaymaster had danced with Peale on Christmas Eve.

"That came the day after our party from Wo-o-o Feelings," Julie said. "Aunt had it up in her room, but she didn't like it there."

"Well, he's not cheap, is he?" Neal said.

My mother was lucky if Darwin Duke showed up with a wilted African violet from the supermarket wrapped in green tinfoil. I remembered that for her birthday he'd given her six white roses, one of which he'd filched for his buttonhole.

We hung up our wet coats in the cloakroom. I took my Kodak from my coat pocket and hung it around my neck. Neal sat down to unlace his boots while I walked out to the orchid tree. I wanted a look at the white card dangling from one of the branches.

> *Thou the idol; I the throng—*
> *Thou the day and I the hour—*
> *Thou the singer; I the song!*
> *(from Gilbert and Sullivan's* Iolanthe,
> *as you no doubt know.)*
> *Here's to more duets!*
> *Dar.*

Dar?

"E.C.?" Neal called to me. "Let's go change. I want to talk to you. Julie says there are swim trunks in all sizes downstairs."

We headed toward the stairs to the pool, Neal in his stocking feet.

Neal said, "Julie's going to bring the bacon and eggs to the galley in The Dome, so I can make us breakfast while the fireworks go off."

"Shouldn't we help her carry things?"

"No. She knows I want to talk to you." He had a small blue backpack over his shoulders. He said it was just "some stuff" to decorate our party.

There were two changing rooms before you reached the pool. We went into the one with the gold M on the door. A family of five could have found happiness there. There was a sitting room with television, a small kitchen, a shower room, a bathroom, a library, on and on.

Ricky Martin's old "She's All I Ever Had" came from somewhere. Julie must have turned on the Bose system.

Neal began undoing the long row of brass buttons.

As I searched for swim trunks my size, I felt like asking him if he'd brought the lighter he'd said he'd return.

"I like her a lot, E.C.," Neal said.

"I figured you did."

"I *really* like her."

"*But?*" I knew one was coming.

"But not in a romantic way. Not that way."

"I was wondering."

"She's not my type, E.C."

"Who said she was?"

"I'm shallow. I like beautiful. I like 36C. I like long legs."

"No one's forcing you."

"I know that."

He was taking off his pants. There was a Santa Claus riding in a sleigh across his undershorts.

"But she's one of the nicest girls I've ever met," he said.

"Me too."

"So we can all have fun together, right?"

"It's okay with me. I don't know if it's okay with her."

"It's okay with her. It's even easier for her, I think."

"I suppose you have a theory about it."

If he heard me, he didn't smile. "I think you defuse things," he said. "I think she's as nervous as I am, for the very opposite reason. She's trying to be cool because she's attracted to me, and I'm trying to be cool because I'm not attracted to her . . . not that way."

"Can I ask you something, Neal?"

"Sure. Shoot."

"Why did you want us all to spend New Year's together?"

"You're my best buddy. She's new and interesting. And I love it here! I used to come here with my father when I was a kid, when the Evanses owned it. It brings back a lot of memories."

I grabbed one of the white towels with the blue S's on it. "I just hope you can handle it if she falls for you."

"She's not the hysterical type or anything, I don't think."

"No, she's quiet and she's shy, but what I meant was don't hurt her. You know?"

Neal took a towel, too. He said, "You're not still pissed at me, are you?"

"For what?"

"Pocketing the little souvenir."

"It's a sucky habit, Neal."

Julie called in, "Did you find suits that fit?"

❄   ❄   ❄

It was Julie's idea to swim *after* we ate.

The Dome was at the top of a winding stairway leading up from the oval pool with the bright-blue water and the S made of white tiles at the bottom.

All the sides of The Dome were glass, and there was more glass when the rounded roof rolled back. More light snow, more stars, and the smoky-looking moon.

My feet sank into the soft white galley carpet, which was wall-to-wall.

"Signs Following" came over the sound system. Julie began describing how Kate Campbell had come to write the song after reading a book about this religious group that believed in snake handling.

She loved the stories behind songs, loved anything to do with what gave musicians or artists their ideas.

Among the things Neal had brought in his backpack was a boxed set of "Fruit Tree," most of the recordings Nick Drake made before he was found dead in bed. Neal claimed that on Drake's nightstand there was a copy in French of Camus's *The Myth of Sisyphus* and on the turntable a recording of Bach's Brandenburg Concertos.

"He was a genius!" Neal said. "Dark as they come: a guitarist, singer, composer . . . and he died age twenty-six, 1974, probably a drug overdose."

"Another one for the dude with the scythe," I told Julie.

Then Neal asked us to listen to Drake's "Know," a song

built on simple blues riffs with only four lines. One line would say to know you were loved, the next one would say to know you weren't, that sort of thing, know I'm here, know I'm not. Nick Drake's voice was this wistful whisper.

"He sounds so frail," Julie said.

"He was tall and lanky," Neal said. "I've read a lot about him.

"Tall and lanky and fascinating, like *you*," Julie said.

"Oh, no, gawd, not like me! The guy was real shy and real smart. He went to Cambridge. He played reeds, piano, and guitar. He was suicidal, and sometimes so depressed he went back to live with his parents and stay in his old room and play nothing but classical music."

Neal had brought paper hats for us. Julie's was red with a black plume. The plume kept falling into her face, and she'd brush it aside or try blowing it away out of the corner of her mouth.

She told us that Crystal Calldownthemoon had written some songs, too, that Nick Drake's titles sounded like hers. "He wrote 'Pink Moon,' and my Mom wrote 'Red, Red Moon.' He wrote 'Time of No Reply,' and she wrote 'Point of No Return.'"

Neal sat listening intently and shaking his head, murmuring, "They do, they do."

I remembered Julie's telling me about having a good listener way at the top of her wish list.

"Shall we read our things while we eat?" Neal asked Julie.

"Oh, migosh, I forgot to tell you, Eddie. Neal wanted us to have something we'd share. A song or a poem—"

"A thought, anything to start us in the New Year," Neal said. "Easy can improvise."

"I have a poem," I said. The chicken poem was in my coat pocket. I hadn't read it again since Mom had handed it to me after lunch.

I went to get it, and when I came back, Neal was frying bacon with Julie leaning against the wall watching him. She was smoking one of Neal's strawberry bidis, as if she always smoked little brown smelly cigarettes.

"Since when?" I asked her.

"It's not really smoking," Julie said. "They don't stay lit."

Julie looked like a kid in her swimsuit, playing dress-up in her red hat. She'd put one of her aunt's cashmere cardigans on. It hung past her knees. Her legs and arms were long and skinny for someone so short, and she had no bust at all. Her glasses were sliding down her nose.

Neal had set the small table that was in the center of The Dome. It was white marble, and Neal had brought paper place mats, silver ones, and small paper shot glasses, also silver. He had put a small bunch of violets in a juice glass, which he placed next to a bottle of Malibu rum.

Nick Drake sang "Five Leaves Left," very softly in the

background, while we ate Neal's eggs, scrambled with ched-
dar cheese and chives. We were sitting Japanese style, on
cushions pulled up to the low, square table.

Neal went first, with a poem called "Fate."

> *It's odd to think we might have been*
> *Sun, moon and stars unto each other—*
> *Only, I turned down one little street*
> *As you went up another.*

"So sad," Julie said.

"But that's one of my theories," Neal said.

"You and your theories." Julie gave him the elbow.

"I mean it! It's all serendipity. It's all chance! Life has no
pattern to it, no grand plan. We just roll about in it."

"But we can change things," I said.

"What things?" Neal asked me.

"The way we are," I said. I needled him with my eyes.
"We can change our bad habits."

"Ah, yes, we all have sucky habits," Neal said.

"I know I've changed just since you guys came into my
life," Julie said. "I never had guy friends." She shrugged and
said under her breath, "I never had girl friends, either."

"That's not the message," Neal said. "The message is
we could just as easily have never met. We *wouldn't* have, if
E.C.'s mother didn't do horoscopes."

"Except maybe we were destined to meet," Julie said. "My mother's song 'Point of No Return' was about that. I never heard it sung, but these are the words.

> *"There was a point when we made a point,*
> *There was a reason on the day we met,*
> *There was a time we won't forget.*
> *We were so high on one another,*
> *We were sky high on one another.*
> *Now there's a curtain that's going down,*
> *Now there's that soft, that sorry sound,*
> *Saying so long, 'bye, see you around.*
> *Now there's the point of no return,*
> *Now there is nothing left to learn.*
> *We were so high, we were sky high.*

"Let's hear it for Crystal Calldownthemoon," said Julie.

"No offense," said Neal, "but could she have had a bit of the weed when she wrote that?"

"It's not as spacey as most of her stuff," Julie said.

"Her song is the opposite of what I'm talking about. I'm pushing the powers of uncertainty."

"Whew!" I said. "The powers of uncertainty. That sounds very weedy to me."

I stood up and shot some photographs.

Neal leaned into Julie the way people do when you're

taking pictures of them, throw their arms around each other, that sort of thing, then jump away after the flash.

"I wish you didn't have to go home," Julie said. "I never thought I'd miss Bob, the dachshund, and Mrs. Rosenkrantz, but then I've never been alone here. It's spooky."

"We'll stay over," Neal said.

"Oh, if you only could."

"We will. How about it, E.C.?"

"I have to get up real early, remember. Like five A.M. I have my job."

"What job?" Julie asked.

"He wraps the out-of-town papers, then someone delivers them."

"But leaving early is good," Julie said, "because I don't want Mrs. Parla to see boys up here. In fact, Neal, you have to move the car to the road behind the house soon."

"Done," Neal said. "Right after the swim."

"Who wants to skinny-dip?" Julie said. "I can put the low, low lights on and we'll hardly see each other."

"What's the point of skinny-dipping if we hardly see each other?" Neal asked, laughing.

"Some of us aren't fully developed yet," Julie said.

"Don't hurt E.C.'s feelings," Neal said.

"If we skinny-dip, we've got to check and be sure the surveillance system isn't on," Julie said.

"There's a surveillance system?" Neal asked.

"For when workers are here, and for parties."

"Was it on Christmas Eve?"

"Sure. It's always on for parties."

"Did you see the films of the party?" Neal said.

"No. I never watch them. A lot of times Aunt doesn't either. She has Diego look at them, since he's always on the door, making everyone sign in. Diego's got a memory like a savant. You only have to tell him your name once."

"Did your aunt see the Christmas party film?" I asked Julie.

"Yes, because Diego thought she ought to have a look at the Dutchman protesters. There were a lot of people wearing Dutchman pins, and some Chaly boys blew up the balloons we found in the solarium later. 'Don't Ditch Dutchman.'" Then Julie laughed. "And there were the Butler sisters taking silverware."

I said, "Mildred and Marilyn Butler from Toybucks?"

"Yes. They took some butter knives. But the real mystery is this guy who took a cigarette lighter from the living room alcove and a silver cigarette case from the solarium. The cigarette case belonged to Simon Slaymaster!"

I looked across at Neal and rolled my eyes to the ceiling.

"What's mysterious about him?" Neal said.

"Nobody's ever heard of him. Diego showed Aunt where he signed the guest book. Aunt asked Doctor Duke if he was enrolled at Serenity High. Then Aunt called Chalfont, and she asked the police, but nobody seems to know anyone named Richard Bachman."

"Richard Bachman," I repeated, because my head was computing very slowly. Blame the two shots of coconut rum I'd downed, or blame my reluctance to put two and two together and get three. Get Stephen King, Richard Bachman, then Neal Kraft.

Neal said, "There aren't any Bachmans around here that I know of."

"I know. Aunt looked in the phone book."

Neal sucked on his bidi and said, "Perhaps he was a mirage."

Julie said, "I think Aunt's more worried about the Dutchman protesters. She says you never know when one of them will go too far."

In the distance the cannon outside the Veterans of Foreign Wars sounded.

The sky began to flash with fireworks.

"Happy New Year!" Neal was the first to wish us that.

The chicken poem was forgotten in the burst of rockets and pinwheels and snaptails.

Fifteen

Mom sounded titillated by the champagne. She said, Sure, stay over, and we wished each other happy New Year.

Next thing I knew, The Duck quacked.

"Happy New Year, my dear boy. Ann and I are so disappointed that you couldn't be here with us."

"Same to you," I managed. I wanted to say, Look, beer barrel, I'm a lot of crappy things, but one of them I'm not is your dear boy.

"If you're staying there, maybe I'll bunk in your room, okay?"

I didn't answer him.

"Okay, E.C.?" he persisted.

"Bunk where you want to bunk," I said, and hung up.

❈   ❈   ❈

I watched the fireworks for a while, standing by the kili-fish gliding in and out of their golden castles in the solarium.

I snapped some pictures of them, their brilliant metallic blue, the fins like billowing sails.

I was always torn between wanting to photograph scenes and abstracts or people. Dad had always told me it was hard to do both well. You had to learn what you were best at.

Right before his death, I was heavily into Diane Arbus, who photographed freaks and outsiders. She was Dad's favorite. Our Siamese, Arbus, was named for her, because she had a pure white tail, instead of a dark one, and one white ear.

Diane Arbus had named one of her kids Doon, which was where our Doon's name came from. Dad used to say in our family he named the hairs and Mom named the heir.

I put my camera around my neck and headed down to the basement, known as The Lower Level at Peligro. I was still on the staircase when I heard Julie's wistful, wispy voice over the sound system, reciting the chicken poem I'd left by my plate while I went to phone Mom.

"'Passing a Truck Full of Chickens at Night on Highway Eighty,' by Jane Mead.

What struck me first was their panic.

Some were pulled by the wind from moving
to the ends of the stacked cages,
some had their heads blown through the bars—

and could not get them in again.
Some hung there like that—dead—
their own feathers blowing, clotting

in their faces. Then
I saw the one that made me slow some—
I lingered there beside her for five miles.

She had pushed her head through the space
between bars—to get a better view.
She had the look of a dog in the back

of a pickup, that eager look of a dog
who knows she's being taken along.
She craned her neck.

She looked around, watched me, then
strained to see over the car—strained
to see what happened beyond.

That is the chicken I want to be."

Julie was sitting in one of the blue-and-white-striped canvas chairs and seemed to be wearing only a huge blue-and-white towel. She put the mike down and said, "Hey, only naked bodies are allowed in here!"

I dove into the pool wearing the Peligro trunks.

"Talk about chicken!" Julie called out to me as I swam for the ladder.

I shed the trunks and tossed them at her.

Neal was swimming around in the center of the pool. The water looked dark green, but now and then the lights inside the pool would catch flesh, pubic hair, a gold chain, the black-and-red skull Neal had tattooed on his arm.

I said, "Is that a pessimistic poem or an optimistic one?" My voice echoed in the pool air.

"I love it! It's about surviving!" Julie jumped in, skinny as a plucked chicken herself.

"Surviving?" Neal said when she surfaced. "Surviving the ride to the slaughterhouse? Some poor deluded chicken thinks it might be going someplace."

I told them that Doctor Duke's client had brought it to him, and Neal was on the same side as The Duck.

"Not me," I said. "I'm with Julie."

"Because you two need therapy," Neal said.

Julie cried, "Let's see what you need," and she headed for Neal, underwater, which set him to yowling like Arbus back when she could still go into heat.

Sixteen

Peale's room was on the second floor, across the hall from Julie's.

"Too bad you can't fit into his pajamas," Julie said. "They're so neat! White silk, black silk, red silk."

"I don't wear pajamas."

"*Please!* Don't give me any mental pictures that could cause me to walk in my sleep!"

She opened the door and snapped on the light.

"Where's Neal sleeping?" I asked.

"Probably in the solarium. He says he likes watching the kilifish. Right now he's moving the car. I had him drive down past the Parlas', like my guests are leaving. Then he'll park down on Bull Run Avenue."

"I hope he's ready when I have to leave."

"You know what I loved? When he swept into the party

tonight with his cap on and spun me around the dance floor. Every girl in the room wished she was me. I saw The Sluts give each other looks."

"I thought you were over The Sluts."

"I am. Honest," she said. "Was your mother surprised that you wanted to sleep over?"

"Nope."

"I guess no one in the world thinks of me as a sex object."

"Give it time."

"Good night, Eddie."

"Good night."

The first thing I saw after I closed the door was a TV set with a thirty-seven-inch screen. Well, why did that come as a surprise? If Peale could travel to Texas in his own first-class seat, Peale could watch TV big time.

In his bathroom there was a framed letter of thanks from Tall Trees to Rosalind Slaymaster for her devotion to the annual Garden Party. Before she bought Peligro, the only time anyone saw her in Serenity was mid-June for that fundraiser. Usually it was right there at Peligro, called Evans Above back then.

There was a poorly focused photo of a young girl who must have been Mrs. S. as a kid, standing with a skinny, buck-toothed woman wearing white harlequin glasses. Another photograph that looked as though it had been snapped at the same time: the young girl in a long green dress with a ruffle. Beside her a lanky fellow, grinning, held up two fingers like horns attached to her head.

There were no towels out. When I opened an oak bureau to look for one, I saw a large scrapbook, and on top of that two diaries.

I opened one.

Property of Rose Fitch

I flipped through it.

Over and over again I wonder what my life would have been like if I had stayed at Tall Trees, if Sonny had never found the job at the Dares'. What Fate had in store for me depended on my being there just when I was. I can pinpoint when life changed for me. That voice saying, "Are you the funeral home?"

I remembered Mom telling me that when Rosalind Slaymaster was a kid, she'd lived and worked at The Dare Funeral Home.

The towels were in the next drawer.

I stripped down to the pair of red satin Fubu boxers my mother had given me for Christmas.

Then I carried the scrapbook across to the bed.

I had to be up by five. It would take me a half an hour to reach the country store, where they dumped *The New York Times*, *The Philadelphia Bulletin*, *USA Today*, and *The Wall Street Journal*. I did the sorting and packaging for the fellow who drove around leaving them in driveways.

I got under the covers, found an old movie with the remote, then began looking at the life of Rose Fitch.

—*from* THE DIARY OF ROSE FITCH, JULY 4

He comes in from a car crash on a big drinking night, the way ones my age do: after games, on the Fourth, New Year's Eve, prom night.

Sonny says there was such a stench of booze puke, he had to put Vicks VapoRub up his nose before he touched him.

Sonny is babbling away about how once Corny bought him a Jell-O at The Rainbow Diner if Sonny would sing "Hello, I'm Mr. Jell-O."

I say, "Cornelius Kraft?"

Sonny nods.

So *that's* who our guest is tonight.

Sonny says, "You don't believe people buy me things, I bet, but they do."

I tell Sonny I know darn well people buy him things because he's always asking them to. Sonny's not bashful. When I was a kid at Tall Trees and Sonny would come Sundays to visit, the other kids would complain that he was always on the slide or in the swing.

I'm pouring coffee into the thermos to take back to Mr. Dare, in the Preparation Room. I'm wondering why I don't feel like jumping up and down with what's just been rolled into The Finishing School, as Mr. Dare calls us.

I can almost see Corny Kraft's weasel face. His buck teeth so close to my lips, I feared he'd take a bite of me.

He could get my heart pounding so, I thought it'd break loose from the flesh of my chest, with his bad breath and cruel eyes.

We were in middle school then. Same age, same grade, and he'd be waiting in the same place sometimes twice a week. Just there to put terror in me, laughing like a loon at me shaking all over when he'd come close.

I ask Sonny if he was washed, and Sonny says washed and drained and you don't have to shave him because there's no beard.

Mr. Dare is peeling off his rubber gloves, and he tells me Corny Kraft is the spitting image of his father.

"It could be Kicker Kraft from thirty years ago."

I can't stand the stink in there.

Mr. Dare says if I think that's bad, I should have been there when they brought in the pouch. Says he almost puked himself.

Says he wishes every fine young athlete like Cornelius Kraft could be invited by, right this moment, to see for himself what's waiting for him inside the bottle.

He asks me if I ever saw "this prince" play, and I say honestly I didn't know *that prince* played anything but mean tricks on people.

Mr. Dare says he played football the likes of which Serenity or any other small town hadn't seen played ever!

"I am not a sports fan," I announce.

"Well, he was a prankster when he was younger, and you got the worst of it. . . . But he was a star, Rose! Now look at him."

I ask if I should pour him some coffee and he says no, he is going back to bed for an hour or two. He grinds out his cigar and goes across to fetch his jacket.

He says, "Get under the fingernails now or you'll have a bad time later, then do the rest tomorrow. Open the windows before you go, and let this place air out!"

On our table under the fluorescent lights he doesn't look real. They never do. They look like store dummies, except he has red scratches down his face.

He's come fresh from the Chalfont Junior Prom. His

shiny black shoes are on a chair, with his plaid cummerbund folded and tucked inside one. Beside them is the sterling silver flask engraved CPK, which Mr. Dare has put masking tape on and marked *Police*.

The black tux jacket with the white carnation still in the lapel is hanging above the tubs where Sonny hosed it down. His shirt, socks, and underwear are churning in the washing machine.

Mr. Dare has covered him from the waist down with a plaid blanket. I lift it up a moment and have a look at his limp little sausage.

I take a rough washcloth to his hands and cut his nails down to his fingertips.

Then the stink gets to me, too, so I leave the shop with the thermos of coffee.

Because it is still dark out, I nearly bump into someone on the path back to the shop.

"Excuse me," he says. "My name is Perry Kraft, and I believe you brought my brother here tonight."

I say, "He came in this morning, about two hours ago, and he won't be in the house for a while. Anyways, visiting hours aren't until ten, and it'll take all of that to get him ready for viewing."

He says he knows I'm Rose Fitch and remembers me from school.

I know who he is too. I know he's the older boy, not a

smidgen like his brother's been. He plays the clarinet in the school band, and piano solos sometimes for assembly. Tight, curly blond hair and one of those who stand up so straight, he looks like some kind of soldier.

He is always in the library, where I go between classes and whenever I want to get away from trouble.

He wears rimless glasses like he is the studious type.

He explains he didn't come by to see his brother, and then I notice he's carrying stuff. He says it's boxers, a suit, shirt, and tie.

I say, "Didn't Sonny remember to get those things?"

He says his mother and daddy were too upset. He's on the verge of bawling himself. I never get over the way it starts in the voice, then the face begins slowly crumpling, so close to the look you get when you're laughing hard, then you see no, that's not laughing.

In the light from the garage roof I see him controlling it. Bites his lip.

He says his grandfather Kraft was here just six months ago, and I tell him I remember that.

He says, "Cornelius was named for him."

I start walking along, and he walks with me.

He tells me, "This is a real rough time for Daddy."

I tell him that it's too bad, things you say to things they say—too bad, is at rest now, out of pain now. Forget the one about a good long life.

Then, Diary, he blurts out, "Daddy said he wished it'd been me."

I say his daddy didn't mean it, and he says, "Yes, he did. He said it right to my face."

"People say things when they're stressed," I say.

He stops walking and stands there crying, taking his glasses off, covering his eyes with his hand.

I touch his sleeve. I tell him when things happen, people just come out with stuff they wish they hadn't.

I tell him I have this coffee I made for Mr. Dare and he could stop in the garage and I'd pour a cup for him.

"No, thank you. You're very kind."

I put the thermos down by the garage door and say I'll take his brother's clothes and see that Mrs. Dare gets them.

Mrs. Dare believes that people in Serenity like to think she dresses their relatives or Mr. Dare does, not the same one you saw out front cutting the hedges or clearing the sidewalks of ice. Not The Corpse Cleaner . . . or his daughter. Never mind, it's always us who snip the nose hairs, put on the pancake, clean out the ears, plug the butt, you name it.

Perry Kraft puts his eyeglasses back on, straightens his shoulders, and asks me if his brother needs his shoes.

I tell him that is left to individual taste.

Then he says he would appreciate it if I didn't spread it

around about what his daddy said, and I tell him I never would.

He shakes his head mournfully and adds, "Not that it'd be news to anyone in Serenity. I guess we'll skip the shoes, Rose."

—*from* THE DIARY OF ROSE FITCH, JULY 16

Who shows up yesterday but Perry Kraft?

It's been about two weeks since we put his brother in the ground.

He's on his Schwinn, and he's got this white carton in his hand.

"I asked Mrs. Dare what you'd like," says he. "I wanted to get you something for being so nice the night my brother . . ." And he can't finish the sentence. He can't face the idea that ferret face croaked.

I tell him I was just doing my job.

I can smell Vitalis on him. I know that smell because we use it sometimes on old men's hair when it won't stay down.

He says he knows how Cornelius used to tease me,

that it was worse than teasing and that was why he telephoned Mrs. Dare to get some ideas what'd please me.

I knew it wouldn't be what I really want, which is a kitty . . . even a puppy. Mrs. Dare always says there is room for only one pet in a funeral establishment, and Littlekitty is it!

So he opens the carton, and inside are two brown-and-blue fish which I never saw anything like. One is mostly brown with blue in it, and one is mostly blue with brown in it.

"They're kilifish," he says.

I tell him, "I don't even have to think what *one* will be named."

"You don't have to name one after me," he says.

I say, "I wasn't going to. I'm giving one the name I always wanted for myself."

He asks me, What is that?

"Rosalind."

I've never told anyone I wanted that name, not even you, Diary.

Perry Kraft gets back on his bicycle, and I run up to show Sonny.

Sonny says he wants the biggest, so I can have the little guy.

I give in and tell Sonny we'll take money from our nest egg for a bowl.

He says he's naming his Kili and he wants Kili to have his own bowl! But I put my foot down and shout, "Even fish need company!"

Today I go by Perry Kraft in the hall, and he says, "Hello, Rosalind," in a low voice I'd be surprised if anybody but me heard.

—*from* THE DIARY OF ROSE FITCH, NOVEMBER 3, #1

I tell Mrs. Dare what's coming up: this thing called
Vocations and Avocations, with everybody in school talking
about one or the other.

She says I could easily say I was learning a vocation
here at The Dare Funeral Home.

I tell her that is all I need to announce to be the
second biggest laughingstock in the school when I am
already the first.

She says, "You may not have the knack of friendship,
Rose, but you have taken a big load off my shoulders."

She says after all these years she is still just a little
finicky about putting rouge on the cheeks of a dead lady.

"It's not work I like, Rose," she says.

I answer her, "Neither one of you likes it. Sonny and me do everything."

She says, "*Me* can't do anything, Rose, but *I* can."

She continues, "I know this conversation is not about grammar, Rose, but about taking Kili and Rosalind to school, so let's get back to it."

"Take them to school for what?"

"For your avocation," she says.

"They just sit in a bowl. They don't *do* anything."

Mrs. Dare claims most people's hobbies don't! People do things to them. She promises to help me.

"My avocation is the care and feeding of my kilifish."

Upper-grade kids are invited for the presentations, and one named Shirley Bryan is going to be trouble.

She is full of nerve and black curls, the one who tap-danced to "Easter Parade" in assembly last April.

You always know the ones who'll go for your throat, same as a dog must when his ruff goes up looking down a street at a little speck on four legs.

"If your kilifish kills something, does it end up at Dare's?" she calls out. Laughter. Of course, *laughter*.

I have only Rosalind with me, since Sonny is afraid for Kili to leave our apartment.

The teacher goes, Shhhhh, to let me finish.

Mrs. Dare has helped me memorize what I am to say

next, about kilifish being closely related to such aquarium fish as the livebearers and the four-eyed fishes and more distantly related to the halfbeaks and the Australian rainbow fishes.

But I get stuck on livebearers. Live comes out fine, but then comes bu, bu, bubu, burr, brra . . .

"Brassiere!" Shirley Bryan starts it. I knew if anybody would, she would.

"Live brassieres!" someone else shouts.

"Rose, take off your brassiere!" a boy yells.

When they want to get you, they get you. No teacher can stop them. No one can.

I hold tightly to Rosalind in the mason jar Mrs. Dare gave me and go back to my seat.

I had read what I had tried to say half a dozen times to both Sonny and Mrs. Dare, never once stuttering.

"Th, th, th, th, that's all, fffffffolks," another boy calls out like Porky Pig at the end of cartoons.

Some kids sing "Row Row Row Your Boat."

"Next!" the teacher calls out over the laughter. "Who is next?" in her angry voice.

Then Perry Kraft shows everyone his copies of Detective Comics and Marvel Comics from 1939 and, after, sits down behind me.

"I'm glad you like your fish, Rosalind," he whispers. "I have discus and rasboras in my aquarium too, but my kilifish are my favorites."

I tell him I gave Sonny one of mine, and he says what a good person I am, that he always knew it.

"He'd have killed Rosalind if I didn't," I whisper back.

Later, I return *Enjoy Your Aquarium* to the library.

There is last year's *Threshold* with a photograph of the marching band sitting on the bleachers in the stadium. Perry Kraft sits ramrod straight, which is his way of sitting. He is in the last row, being so tall, his glasses catching the sun, barely smiling. He bears a resemblance to the famous pianist Van Cliburn.

I rip out the photograph very carefully, fold it, and put it in my wallet.

I know when I come through the door he's done something, and then I see the empty fish bowl sitting on the card table. There is the golden castle we both saved to buy, and the floating fern plantings, but there is no sign of Kili.

Sonny sits there, down in the mouth, so I ask him where Kili is. Don't think I don't know something terrible has happened.

He says, "I thought maybe you took him to school."

I start to blow up, reminding him he didn't want me to take him. I only took Rosalind.

Then he just says right out that Littlekitty got in and took Kili.

"You left the door open!" I yell at him. "That's how Littlekitty got in."

He says he hates Littlekitty and that damned cat can never come here again, tell Mrs. Dare!

I say, "She doesn't want him here in the ninth place! She never did!"

I ask him how many times has she said put him back if he gets in?

Sonny says, "Well he came here, Rose, and that's the end of Kili."

I know he is trying hard not to cry, biting his knuckles. He is this close.

I go across to him, put my arms around his neck, and tell him never mind, it wasn't his fault.

He says, "Littlekitty is a killer!"

I say, "It's not really Littlekitty's fault, either. Cats are made to hunt birds and fish."

He is whimpering now, and I say, "Shhhhh. It's all right, Sonny. We can get another kilifish."

"NO, NEVER!" he shouts.

He whines he was his daddy and I say I know you were.

"And you know I'm yours, too."

I tell him I know that.

Poem to a Certain Someone

You look like Van Cliburn,
But as far as I can discern,
You aren't as happy.
Or is my judgment sappy?
I just wonder if you know
I'm here for you in sun, wind, rain, and snow.

THE GARDEN PARTY at Evans Above

Dear Rose,

 *On June the tenth we are having the annual
Garden Party Fund-Raiser at Evans Above. But
this year we are celebrating the 50th Anniversary
of Tall Trees.*

 *Senator Louis Gaelin is going to attend, and
Mayor Edward Kupper will be on hand as well.*

 *Many Serenity notables will be present for tea
and sandwiches, and a short dance recital given by
Top Hat.*

 Since you are an alumna of Tall Trees, Rose

Fitch, you are invited to be our guest and bring someone.

Please mark the date on your calendar, and I look forward to seeing you that afternoon.

Cordially yours,
Marlin Evans,
Chairman, Board of Directors
Tall Trees

I don't have anything to wear to a garden party, and I don't have anyone to wear it with. Mrs. Dare says she can take care of the what to wear, but I will have to call up Perry Kraft my own self.

"Per-ry Kraft?" I say, like she's said Perry Como or Elvis Presley.

"You defaced public property for a photograph of him"—she laughs—"so it must be very serioso."

"What is serioso," I say, "is you going through my drawers."

"I was looking for Littlekitty," she lies.

I tell her Littlekitty prefers to sleep in coffins, as we

both well know from getting the hairs off guests before the relatives come for a viewing.

Then she plays PK and I play me.

"Hello, Perry?"

"Yes? This is Perry."

"I have an invitation to a party."

She stops me and says, "State the nature of the party *immediately*, its place—its place is *very* important, Rose—and say that there'll be no charge because you are a guest. Then don't pause after you say your name, Rose. Don't give him time to think, and don't act like a mouse! Say your name. State your purpose!"

When I do finally call him, I ask him if he can go to a party at Evans Above on the following Saturday, my treat.

Behind me Mrs. Dare socks her head with her fist and starts whispering that it's not *my treat*. "Take it back, or he'll think you're spending money on him. Say it's free."

But he has already agreed to go, just like that.

He says he has heard about it, and fine, he will come by for me.

"Tell him it's free!" Mrs. Dare whispering harder.

"Fine. Four o'clock? I will expect you then."

Mrs. Dare shakes her head and says, "You never said it was free."

I ask her, "So what? What's the difference?"

"He'll think you're desperate if you have to treat him," she says.

"But he answered yes right away. YES!"

"I know he's not like his brother, Rose, but boys get ideas about girls with big boobs, so watch him."

—*from* THE DIARY OF ROSE FITCH, JUNE 10, #1

It is your perfect June afternoon, warm with sun, and
the ruffle on the dress Mrs. Dare made me is tacky.

Before My First Date Ever arrives, Mrs. Dare says she
wants a picture of her and me in that dress, so Sonny snaps
one. Then she takes one of Sonny and me and he gets silly,
trying to make rabbit ears over my head.

We laugh to beat the band, the three of us.

Perry Kraft has on this blue-and-white-striped seersucker
suit with a white shirt and navy tie, plus white shoes.

I could pass for Quite Okay if she had not got it into
her head to put a ruffle on. I should have seen it was wrong
when I was standing for fittings, but I was too excited over

my first tailor-made article of clothing.

Perry Kraft apologizes for us walking to the Garden Party, because he doesn't like to ask if he can borrow the family car. It just stirs up memories.

I like to walk and don't mind all the nosy faces in this little Peyton Place seeing me with him.

Perry tells me there's this girl, never mind who. She was his brother's date the night of the Chalfont Junior Prom. She asked friends for a ride home because Cornelius was drinking.

"Smart her," I comment.

Perry says his father believes Cornelius would be alive today if she'd stuck with him. "See, Rose, Cornelius was driving carelessly and fast because he was so outraged that she ditched him."

"Who can blame her?"

He says, "Do you think I do? But I would like to talk to her, you know, to find out what she can tell me about his last hours on earth."

I can tell him more.

Tell him I went back after it didn't stink in there, and wiped him down, from his toes up to the curve of his neck, with the little bump of the Adam's apple. Mr. Dare had set his face when he'd first come in.

I used a small diamond file on the sides and tip of each fingernail. Then I took a Q-tip to his ears and nostrils, and Vaseline to his eyelashes. Where the lacerations were sutured, I took hot wax to the scar. Then Max Factor sun beige medium pancake on his face.

I could get his cotton boxers up his waist my own self, but for the rest of it I needed Mrs. Dare or Sonny. I called over the intercom, "Our guest needs casketing!"

I was thinking of you, Perry K., not Corny. Maybe a little of Corny, enough to gloat: I'm here, you're not. . . . I live, you rot. Mr. Dare's little ditty when he's got someone on the porcelain table he doesn't fancy.

"Wow! Rose!" Mrs. Dare about faints. "He looks like he came back from a month's vacation in Miami. You sure did turn the other cheek, honey chile. If he'd done to me what he did to you, I'd have left the boogers up his nose and in his eye corners, and the drool dried on his chin. He'd stay the color of flour, too."

We get his suit on, then fold his hands one over the other.

Mrs. Dare says, "You're going to have to keep those to yourself now, Buster!"

I ask Perry if he's ever been to Evans Above.

"Been there? Ever been there? Marlin Evans is my father's best friend. Tiger Evans and Kicker Kraft, the Penn State Double Threat Halfbacks. They were Dekes together."

"What's Dekes?"

"They were in a fraternity together, Rose."

"How come I'm not Rosalind anymore?"

"Rosalind."

"I like that name."

"Okay . . . " he says, "Rosalind . . . the thing is I'm afraid to even talk to this girl."

"If you're going to keep talking about her, I would just as soon know who she is."

He changes the subject and asks, "Did Mrs. Dare make that dress?"

"How'd you know?"

"I knew someone did."

"It's okay, but the ruffle is funny."

"Rose," he says out of the blue, "you were there for me when I needed you, and I'll always remember you for it. You didn't hear me hesitate a second when you asked for this favor."

"Did I call it a favor?"

"I don't remember how you put it, Rose."

"*Rosalind.*"

"Rosalind. That night my brother died was the worst night of my life."

"You already gave me the kilifish for that night is what I thought."

"So I have to be there for you, Rosalind."

"Well, thanks, Perry."

"I still miss my—"

"Your brother, Perry? You miss Cornelius?"

"Daddy is who I miss."

"Where'd he go?"

"No place, Rose. He's just not himself now."

Ahead of us there are barriers in the driveway and police directing traffic.

I say, "We would have had trouble parking even if you could have gotten the family car."

"She'll probably be here."

"Who?"

"I told you. My brother's girlfriend."

I see other girls in ankle-length skirts too, but not with ruffles.

My dress is green to match my eyes, and the ruffle is gold-green from Nolan's Notions, with a spiderweb design.

Perry asks what about me? Have I ever been to Evans Above before?

"No, but on the invitation Mr. Evans seemed to know me."

"Oh, Rose."

"He did, Perry!"

"It's what I love about you, Rose."

"What?"

"Your innocence."

I throw my head back and laugh hard. "If you knew the stuff I have to do back in the shop, you wouldn't think so, Monsieur Kraft."

The French just happened.

—from THE DIARY OF ROSE FITCH, JUNE 10, #2

"Well, hel-lo there, Perry!"

A slim old man in a bow tie smiles up from the table where there is a glass jar with $5 in it.

I nudge Perry, telling him it's free for us.

"Hello, Mr. Evans." Perry goes about his business as though I haven't spoken. He says, "This is someone who's been very kind to our family, name of Rose Fitch. Rose, this is Mr. Evans."

"Hello, Rose. Your name reminds me that tomorrow our daughter is coming home from Switzerland, where she attends Le Rosey."

"What's that?"

Perry laughs hard as though I'd made a joke, and explains,

"Institut le Rosey is a prep school . . . a rather famous one."

"I never understood why your father didn't send *you* away, Perry, get you the hell out of here so you weren't reminded of your brother every day." Mr. Evans is lighting a Virginia Round, which he keeps in a long ivory holder.

"I'm doing fine," Perry Kraft assures him, and he reaches in his back pants pocket for his wallet.

"It's free," I whisper up at his face.

Perry is removing ten dollars from his wallet.

"Per-ry!" I pull the sleeve of his seersucker jacket.

"What, Rose?"

"It's free. Free to me and my guest." I look at Mr. Evans for confirmation. "Remember? You wrote me a letter."

Perry smiles down at me. "It's for a good cause, Rose."

"Tell him you invited me, Mr. Evans. Remember? You said you'd see me and a guest."

"Oh, yes, of course, Rose, Rose,—"

"Fitch! Rose Fitch!"

Perry begins to pull me along. "Come on. We don't want to hold up the line."

"There's no line! . . . He didn't remember he wrote me."

Perry lets go of my arm. "He remembered, Rose. . . . Why do you keep looking down?"

"It's the ruffle. It doesn't belong on this kind of dress."

"What you want to remember is— Oh, Lord. Lord. There she is."

131

"What is it I want to remember?"

"Oh, Lord, there she is."

"That girl Corny dated?"

"Shhhhh! *Rose.*"

"*Where* is she?"

"She could hear us, Rose."

He is red, his poise is shot. Perspiration appears above his lips.

"What is it I want to remember? You never finished the sentence, Perry."

"What *was* it?" He hits his forehead with his fist.

"Search me."

"Ah! I know. I remember."

"What?"

"You want to remember that looking down at the ruffle all the time is worse than just having a ruffle you don't like, because you look like a chicken hunting ground bugs."

I get angry at the picture he makes in my mind, of me clucking along like some chicken. "What's the *matter* with you?"

"Maybe this wasn't such a nifty idea," he mumbles, turning his head as though he's saying it to the air, not to me.

But I am skilled at hearing things not meant for my ears.

People who are talked about behind other people's hands acquire that talent.

It makes me determined to get that ruffle *off!*

—*from* THE DIARY OF ROSE FITCH, JUNE 10, #3

While the dancers from Top Hat get ready to perform,
I go inside Evans Above and follow a series of cardboard
arrows painted red, pointing to a downstairs bathroom.

I look everywhere for a scissors, but all I can find are
neat vellum-lined drawers in marble-topped cabinets with
white wood-paneled doors and gold rosette knobs.

Sure that in this house there is such a thing as The
Sewing Room, I hurry up the staircase and down the hall,
opening and closing doors. There are beds in all the rooms,
and there is not a Singer sewing machine in sight anywhere.

Then I see what has to be the master bedroom,
enormous and antique, dark except for the tiny lamp on
the dresser with gold-flecked fringe hanging from the

shade. There is the old, lovely smell of gardenia in the room, and a grand canopy bed.

I would have liked to stretch out with my feet up just long enough to imagine myself mistress of that house, napping.

But I do not want to leave Perry alone too long, or be gone long enough for him to think I am sick somewhere sitting on a toilet, which Mrs. Dare said happened to her on her first movie date. She was so excited, she said, that she got the trots, never dreaming the Dare boy with the big ears who took her to see Clark Gable for the first time had a corpse in his parlor.

Things people keep in bedroom drawers: cigarettes, lighters, matchbooks from ritzy restaurants (The Canal House—hoo hoo, get you). Pills. Combs. Revlon. Shoelaces. Flashlight. Where are some scissors?

I hear her voice before I am face-to-face with Shirley Bryan.

I hear her call to someone, "I'll change in here."

I look up from the chest of drawers I've been rifling through to hear Shirley say next, "What are you doing in here, Rose Fitch?"

"What are *you* doing in here?" I ask her right back, everything inside me sinking because I know I'm not going to come out of this room as easy as I came into it.

Shirley Bryan states that she is changing into her

costume and *you*, she says, looking daggers at me, are stealing!

"Stealing what?" I answer in a disgusted tone, but next the door has opened again, and before I can blurt out, Oh, listen, I just want to find a scissors and cut off my ruffle, Shirley Bryan is already in the doorway shouting that she found a thief!

Then Mrs. Bryan, sublimely sleek owner of Top Hat, waiting in the hall for her daughter on an antique bench, jumps to her feet and trills, "Someone call security, *please!*"

"No one's going to search me!" I shout once I'm outside again.

"Rose? Rosalind, please keep your voice down."

Two men in white suits, white shirts, black ties, and tight little mean smiles appear, one on either side of me.

One smiles. "Just the purse, Miss Fitch. No need for a scene."

"No!"

"Rosalind?" says Perry. "Just open it and show them you have nothing in there that is Evans property."

"N . . . O! I am not a thief! I happen to know the bitch who says I am is stupid Shirley Bryan! Go through *her* purse!"

Perry's face turns the color of the red in summer sunsets, and he's sprouted a hive under one eye, nickel size.

135

"Shhhh, Rose! Don't say her name so loud!"

It takes me all of a dumb minute to figure out Shirley Bryan is the one Corny was with that night, the very one whose name Perry won't tell me.

"Testing . . . testing. One, two, three, okay? TOP HAT IS PROUD TO PRESENT MISS SHIRLEY BRYAN DANCING THE DANCE OF THE SUGAR PLUM FAIRY FROM *THE NUTCRACKER*."

And that dizzy music begins, *Ta tee ta ta ta tee ta ta ta* . . .

"Perry? Take me home?"

"Rose, Rosalind, I came here to see her."

"*Who?*"

"Shirley."

While that is registering, one of the Evans Above security guards grabs the purse from my hand and puts his fingers inside.

I hang on his arm and hit his chest with my fist.

"Give me that!" I'm shouting at the top of my lungs.

Now Mr. Marlin Evans comes hobbling down the length of the lawn.

Rats desert the sinking ship. Perry Kraft moves away, gets lost in the crowd before the bandstand.

The music tinkles in the air, and out comes Shirley in blue chiffon, up on toes, fingers fluttering.

Applause.

"Now, Rose Fitch," says Mr. Evans in a quiet and

reasonable voice, "even events that are free require a certain decorum."

One of the men in the white suits hands my purse back to me.

There are people who aren't watching Shirley Bryan. They are the ones watching me.

Mr. Evans states it would be nice if I was quiet while a fellow student of mine from Serenity High School performs for everybody.

I tell him, "What would be nice would be if you didn't accuse a guest of taking stuff! I never took anything that didn't belong to me in my entire life!"

"No need to shout, Rose. Boys?"

All the while Mr. Evans talks to me, he has this sweet smile on his face as if we're quietly discussing the fact that The Rainbow Diner has just raised the price of pie to thirty cents a slice, a dime extra for à la mode.

The white suits hold me by the elbows and are walking me toward the driveway, my feet off the ground, tears starting with snorting noises behind them if I don't get out of there in time.

I don't.

—from THE DIARY OF ROSE FITCH, SAME AWFUL DAY

There is a pleasure to seeing your home before your eyes when you have come from someplace you weren't wanted, or welcome.

Even if it is the tacky upstairs of the Dare garage, next to the storage room stacked with caskets, plant stands, urns, and rollers.

I feel my heart lift as I come near. I see the minivan with the tinted windows in the driveway. Perhaps someone new has come. I see Mrs. Dare out watering the rosebushes in the front and wonder what has gotten into her, since she claimed only I should do that or Sonny, never the proprieters out front with the hose! It didn't look businesslike.

Suddenly I am glad they have such a business! All the

town, sooner or later, ends up on the porcelain table out in the shop, all of them who count, anyway . . . all the ones who looked down their noses at me just a while ago.

Your name reminds me that tomorrow our daughter is coming home from Switzerland, where she attends Le Rosey.

Your name is Asshole and it reminds me that you forget who you invite to your parties! You say they're free, then take ten dollars!

You stink and stink, Mr. Smiley Evans!

I can feel the humiliation like a line made across my forehead with a knife point, feel as though I could bleed shame into my own hands like blood, feel it behind my eyes where I ache from crying, and feel it in my knees, wanting to sink into some soft ground and never get up after. Stay on my knees like some dumb statue praying life will end right now because I have had it up to here!

But now I am home. I think of the Dares' as home this early evening, and it looks good to me, because it is familiar. Here I know what is expected of me.

"Rose! Oh, Rose! I've been out here waiting for you, honey!"

"What's the matter?" I feel only a little disappointed, because whatever is the matter will postpone the telling of the Garden Party fiasco. *Just open your purse.* God! Shivers go up and down my back. . . . Were they laughing at the ruffle on my dress, too?

"Rose, something awful has happened! Sonny has to go before Mr. Dare gets home!"

"Go where? Shall I send him down to Rainbow?"

"No!" Mrs. Rose shakes her head so adamantly, the white harlequin glasses move down her nose and she shoves them back in a brusk gesture. "Sonny has to live somewhere else."

"Why?"

"You come with me now. You're the only one who can do this. I can't do it. I can't let Mr. Dare even see it, honey, for he would kill Sonny."

"What?" I keep saying, hardly aware how fast Mrs. Dare is pulling me along, down past the van, in where the Fleetwoods are and the hearse, then up the stairs.

"Just go on in there and take care of it, Rose."

She is crying. As long as I have known her, I have never seen her cry.

"I'll take care of it, whatever it is," I assure her, and I feel good about someone waiting for me, and needing me.

Whatever Sonny did, well, Mrs. Dare would take it back about him not living there any longer. They could not operate The Dare Funeral Home without Sonny.

I open the door and see Sonny at the card table.

He is sitting there white and glum with his hands folded.

Then I glimpse what is inside the fishbowl, all curled up, face squashed against the glass, eyes wide open, tail hair fanned against some seaweed, horrified and dead, paws pressed down on the golden sea castle. A large cement block holds the tin cover on.

"This time he got Rosalind, Rose. He sneaked in through the door, and before I knew it, he had her in his mouth."

"Oh, Sonny. What have you done to Littlekitty?"

"I had to drown him, Rose, because he killed Rosalind. And before that he killed Kili. He is a killer, you know."

From outside the door Mrs. Dare calls, "Rose? Please be quick! Mr. Dare's due back at any moment!"

"Don't tell him!" I open the door. "Why does he have to know what Sonny did? I'll bury Littlekitty and we can say he's strayed."

"Littlekitty doesn't do that." Mrs. Dare is wringing her hands.

"I told him already," Sonny says, "when he called to see if we needed something. I told him Littlekitty's drowned."

"What did he say?"

"He said I told that cat not to go swimming."

"He had a few," Mrs. Dare says. "He didn't believe you."

—*from* THE DIARY OF ROSE FITCH, FOURTH OF JULY

Fourth of July Mrs. Dare gets the idea to have a picnic with me at Dutchman Park, and we would ask Sonny.

I make the egg-and-olive sandwiches with the crusts cut off that Sonny loves, and Mrs. Dare brings macaroni and potato salads, huge sour pickles, slices of salami and bologna, and a box of Mallomars, which are Sonny's favorite cookie.

We leave Mr. Dare covering the phone in the casket selection parlor, where he prefers sitting since there are no windows people can look in. He sits in the dark, in the oak Morris chair, in his underwear, drinking port. He is still inconsolable over the demise of Littlekitty, made worse by the adoption of Mary from the Animal Rescue Farm.

Mary is a fat, green-eyed white cat who cares little for

people dead or alive and spends most of her days asleep under furniture or eyeing us from high places.

"I think he would like to take Mary back to ARF," I tell Sonny as we sit on the auto robe at Dutchman Park, "but he is afraid it will look bad, since he signed the adoption papers the very day after Littlekitty died."

I wear a red-and-white pinafore Mrs. Dare has outgrown and sport a new tight curly Toni permanent Mrs. Dare has given me.

Sonny is thinner even than his usual thin self. His sandy hair stands up as though it has a hair dryer aimed at it, with Sonny's large hands patting it before he puts his fingers in his mouth to bite hangnails.

"Mr. Dare was so eager to have something to replace Littlekitty," says Mrs. Dare, in her white silk patio suit to match her harlequins. Her high-heeled slippers sink into the park grass and make walking hard. "Mary will come around in time. She just needs to feel at home."

"Littlekitty was a killer," says Sonny.

"*You're* the killer, Sonny!" Mrs. Dare shouts at him. "If you hadn't of killed that poor cat, we'd be back to normal instead of you down living in '85' and Rose by herself!"

"How do you like '85,' Sonny?" I ask him. "Do you get enough to eat?"

"Louie Miller plays the radio too loud. I tell him to turn it down, but he doesn't pay attention to me."

"Louie Miller better watch out," Mrs. Dare says under her breath, "or he'll be floating somewhere."

"Do you miss me?" I ask him.

"Guess what, Rose! I'm learning to play checkers!"

"He doesn't have those emotions, Rose," says Mrs. Dare.

"Of course he does!"

"Louie Miller is teaching me checkers"—Sonny punches the air—"and he can get me a job at the A&P, too."

"The Peroskis aren't as good as you, Sonny," I tell him. "He can't even do incisions, so Mr. Dare's back to doing them all."

"*She's* good," says Mrs. Dare. "She married down, in my opinion, way, way down. He's nothing but a pretty boy with muscles, but at least he can lift bodies easy as a roach filching a breadcrumb."

"Sonny's worth more than the two of them put together!" I say.

"The Peroskis will learn. Just be glad they don't want to live in the apartment."

"Just be glad I'm still there to cover up their blunders!" I put in.

"The Peroskis will learn," Mrs. Dare says again, as if she can convince herself by repeating it.

Sonny makes that sucking noise he always does at the end of sipping soda through a straw, gets up, and starts off, not a word to me or Mrs. Dare.

"Where's *he* going?" Mrs. Dare asks.

I say, "His feelings are hurt. We shouldn't talk about the Peroskis, because he gets jealous."

"Feelings you call it? Honey, you asked him if he missed you and he starts talking about some board game he's learning!"

"He has feelings, Mrs. Dare."

"And look over there, speaking of feelings, look, Rose."

Three trees down, on their own blanket, are Shirley Bryan and Perry Kraft.

I have not spoken to him since a year ago at Evans Above.

They must have said *something* to Sonny, for he has stopped to talk to them.

And to sing.

"Yes, he's going to!" Mrs. Dare exclaims.

What does Sonny have on? I cringe, suddenly noticing his clothes, seeing them through their eyes. He wears some light-blue one-piece thing, like a child's thin playsuit, unironed, just a slit for a fly, and he isn't wearing anything under it including underwear.

Perry Kraft is swinging his finger like a baton, while Sonny begins:

> *"Hel-lo, I'm Mr. Jell-O,*
> *I cannot read nor write . . ."*

—*from* THE DIARY OF ROSE FITCH, JULY 4, #2

"I don't know day from night,
I'm a strange fel-low
I'm Mis-ter Jell-O,
Hel-lo! Hel-lo! Mis-ter Jell-O!"

"Well, hi, Rose. I'm Shirley Bryan."

"I know who you are."

"Nice to see you, Rose."

"Hello, Perry."

"Sonny offered to sing 'Hello, I'm Mr. Jell-O' for us if we'd give him a quarter."

"They gave me a dollar, Rose, because they said I was

worth more than twenty-five cents, which is the same as a quarter."

"You like to entertain, don't you, Sonny?" Perry Kraft asks him.

"I'm learning checkers," Sonny answers.

"I play checkers," Perry Kraft says. "I'll play with you sometime."

"Will you treat me to The Sleepy Lagoon?"

I speak up sharply. "You have your own money, Sonny."

"I lost my good job at the Dares'."

"The Sleepy Lagoon ride petrifies me!" From Shirley Bryan.

"I'm not scared of it," Sonny tells her. "I've never been on it."

Shirley Bryan giggles. She says to me, "He's a pistol! We love your brother!"

I say, "He's not my brother. He's my father!"

"Your father?" She gulps.

I put my hand firmly on Sonny's arm. "Sonny, Mrs. Dare made a picnic for you, and it would be nice if you came back to our blanket and enjoyed it with us."

"I miss you," he says.

"That's so sweet!" Shirley Bryan coos.

"Come on, Sonny. Come with me."

"I'm going to the Lagoon, Rose."

"Please don't, Sonny. We went to all this trouble for you."

Perry Kraft is on his feet, smoothing his hands down his white ducks, taking my arm. "Can I say something, Rose?"

"It's a little late for a heart-to-heart talk, Perry Kraft."

I get my arm back from his fingers.

"Rose, don't hang on to injuries. I've learned from experience it's best to let go old grievances. . . . Now, Rose, we'd like to be your friends, not have this hostility on your part."

He looks down at me, smiling, while I think how would *we* like it if *we* both got spit in *our* faces?

He says, "Why, when Shirley said her name to you, she would be dead if looks could kill. There's no rhyme or reason for that, Rose."

"Come on, Sonny!" I shout it angrily.

"And that's another thing, Rose. When someone is trying hard to be nice to your father, why do you step in and act like someone is being unkind to him?"

"Because he's not a performing monkey! He came on a picnic with *us!*"

I turn and point to our auto robe, where Mrs. Dare sits amidst all the food, watching us through her white harlequins, now raising one hand and wiggling one finger, mouthing, "Hel-lo!"

When I turn back, Sonny is gone.

I am in tears now.

"Rose," says Perry Kraft, "why don't you go back and enjoy your picnic? I bet I know where he ran off to."

"It doesn't take a giant intellect to know he's at The Lagoon."

"See how you are, Rose? That's hostile. And you know what I was about to say? I'll go look for him. Shirley and I are going to take a walk anyway, and we'll treat him—"

"*You'll* treat him," Shirley Bryan interrupts. "I'm afraid of that ride."

Perry Kraft nods. "*I'll* treat him, then we'll send him back to your blanket. How's that?"

"Don't do me any favors. Your favors don't turn out to be favors."

I have already turned and started back to the auto robe when I hear her say, "That ungrateful bitch! Who the hell does she think she is?"

FREAK ACCIDENT AT DUTCHMAN KILLS LOCAL MAN

Sonny Fitch, 46, of Elmer Evans House at 85 Forge Avenue, was killed on Fourth of July afternoon at Dutchman Park.

Mr. Fitch had apparently entered The Sleepy Lagoon in a boat by himself, the last one on the line, and when the boat came out of the winding tunnel, it was empty.

Mr. Fitch could not swim.

A couple in the boat ahead of him said he was leaning into the water, trying to catch the giant goldfish on display under the lights there.

There were reports that he had been offered

several "Jell-O shots" by a large party picnicking nearby, as a reward for singing. These "shots" contain vodka, and though they seem fairly innocent, they are lethal when swallowed in large numbers. The belief is that Fitch was also "treated" to the boat ride.

A native of Serenity, Mr. Fitch grew up at Tall Trees and then entered a training program that allowed him to live at "85" while he worked at Holy Family Hospital.

Later, he and his only survivor, a daughter named Rose Fitch, became employees of The Dare Funeral Home, where they also lived.

Services for Mr. Fitch will take place there at 6 P.M. tomorrow evening.

Dear Rose,

I feel the necessity to tell you what I told the police regarding your father's death. Perhaps they have already spoken with you.

First, I want to assure you that I was not one of the ones who gave Sonny Jell-O shots. You can ask Shirley and she will verify that we did not reach The Sleepy Lagoon area until after that happened.

Sonny so liked to entertain people that I did not discourage him from singing the little song Cornelius made up for him to sing. No one, believe me, poked fun at him, for Sonny was our own local character and much loved, as you know, Rose.

Sonny spoke to me about the killifish, which he could not seem to forget, and right before I bought the ticket for The Sleepy Lagoon for him, he asked if fish were in the water there.

Rose, I admit that I do not sleep easily nights knowing I had this discussion with him and let him go on the ride alone. But believe me that then I did not know he had been fed alcohol.

I have always admired you, Rose, for making the best of what the good Lord gave you in this life. I hope you can continue down that path.

Sincerely,
Perry Kraft

—*from* THE DIARY OF ROSE FITCH, APRIL 11

"Are you the funeral home?"

"Yes. This is Dare's."

"Let me speak to a Dare then."

"There are none here at the moment. May I help you?"

More and more in the year since Sonny died, they are not here.

Mr. Dare drinks two towns away at The Drop Inn, where he
imagines no one knows him. She spends her days at her sister's
store, Steph's Stuff, the two of them on a couch in the back,
eating bagels or pizza or Chinese takeout, while customers paw
through the novelties and ask How much?

"If there's nobody in charge there, how in damnation
hell am I going to get my sister down to you and arrange
for her cremation?"

"If you tell me where your sister is, I can have her brought here. Then this evening Mr. Dare will be in, and you can talk with him."

If he can still talk. Last January he was arrested for Driving While Intoxicated, as he returned another cat who wasn't right to ARF.

"My sister works, did work, in your hospital. We haven't seen Selma in years and years. Then a stranger calls and says she's dead of an aneurysm."

"I'm so sorry. Where is she now?"

"She's somewhere called Two Pastures off Sheep Road. Know where that is?"

"No, but I don't have to know. Mr. Peroski drives the coach, and he'll find it."

"Who's Mr. Peroski?"

"He's Mr. Dare's assistant."

"Who're you?"

"I am the receptionist, Rose Fitch, and also an assistant cosmetician."

—Rose, I don't have my heart in helping anyone pick out a casket.

—Mrs. Dare, you never did have your heart in much around here and were lucky to have me and Sonny. But now if you don't show the caskets, your heart is out of here altogether. I'm left with the dirty work!

—Dirty work? Helping someone who's lost a loved one?

—Just who I don't want to make a sales pitch to!

—If you do that for me, I'll talk to Mr. Dare about making you The Pre-Need Counselor.

—I don't want to sell caskets!

But I know they are in a sweat over Call Casket, a new radio pitch from a Vermont coffin carpenter who ships by mail.

"Hello? Hello? Are you still there? My name is Simon Slaymaster."

"How do you do, Mr. Slaymaster."

"How do I do? I'm lonesome as hell, if you want to know. I've come from Texas to bury my twin, and I don't even know where to get a good meal in this town."

"You go to The Canal House, sir."

"How about you going with me?"

"I'd feel funny, sir. I don't even know you."

"Is there someone there who can answer the phone?"

"Mrs. Peroski can answer the phone."

That's about all Mrs. Peroski can do. When she delivers a guest from Preparation to Viewing, the corpse is always overrouged. She is finicky giving shampoos and sometimes skips them. Her manicures are sloppy.

"Then I'll come by in a taxi and pick you up! What's the name again? Ruth? Rose?"

"Rosalind, Mr. Slaymaster."

Dinner at The Canal House! A first for yrs. truly.

—*from* THE SCRAPBOOK OF ROSE FITCH,
LARGE POSTCARD OF THE EIFFEL TOWER,
PARIS, FRANCE

The Dare Funeral Home
Aquetong Road
Serenity, Pennsylvania
U.S.A.

Dear Mrs. Dare,
Now I wish I'd taken French instead of Spanish
at SHS. (Remember it was you who said take
Spanish because we're a lot more likely to have a
Hispanic guest than a French one?)
Now I sure could use French, because neither

Simon or me knows boo about what they're saying here. We stay here one more day, then go to Venice, Florence, Rome—home! Which is Texas for me now. I've gotten to love the darn place!

Please let me know if any small buildings come up for sale in the downtown business section, since Simon wants to buy me a first-anniversary gift and tells me I'm right about real estate being a good investment.

Tell Mr. Dare hello.

Love,

Rosalind Slaymaster, known to you as Rose.

P.S. Please save this for me, for my scrapbook.

—*from* THE DIARY OF ROSE FITCH, DECEMBER 5

One way Simon and I are not alike (so many ways we are!) is that he dreams every night and I seldom do.

When I do, I am involved in one of the old routines: inserting the rounded plastic disks in the cadaver to keep the eyelids from sinking, or sewing the mouth shut after the formation is satisfactory.

The only living person ever in my dreams is Sonny. I never remember what he does in the dream, or if he speaks, but I know he needs me. His hand is extended, the long fingers, the nails he was often slow to cut. I take his hand and it is cold, as though he has rigor mortis. I wake up remembering Yes, he's dead.

Across from me this cool, peaceful night on the ranch,

my husband reads the newspaper, while I watch *Monday Night Football*.

I answer the phone when it rings.

"Hello, Rose?" the man says, and I know from the "Rose" he's someone from my past.

"Yes, this is Rose."

"This is Alex, Rose. I called to tell you Faye died."

"Who? Who died?"

"Faye, Rose. Faye Dare."

"Mr. Dare?"

"It's me, Rose."

"I never called her Faye—that's why you stopped me."

"She had an asthma attack and it was bad. Remember the way she couldn't get her breath after she'd brush Littlekitty's hairs from a casket?"

"Yes, I do."

"It was that kind of struggle to get her breath. I purposely got a Siamese from Petland so there wouldn't be much hair, but now I believe it's the dander, not the hair. The asthma took her heart out, Rose."

"I'm sorry to hear that."

"I knew you would be. You two were thick."

"Will there be a service, Mr. Dare?"

"She didn't want anything. I'm going to put the cremains out under her rosebushes."

"Thank you for telling me, Mr. Dare."

"She liked you, Rose. You and Sonny. Those were happy days, weren't they?"

"Thanks for calling, Mr. Dare."

—*a gift tag from* THE SCRAPBOOK OF ROSE FITCH, 1983

*Merry Christmas, Babes. This little man is named
after my favorite preacher, Norman Vincent Peale.
He wants to live with you.
He'll bring you luck, just wait and see. SSS.*

Seventeen

Neal poked his head in the door. "You're not asleep. I couldn't sleep, either."

I put the diary down and said, "Want to go?"

"Don't you have another hour before work?"

"I'll go home first, put my jeans on."

I wasn't going to mention the diaries or the scrapbook. I had the idea if I told him there were things in them about his father, he'd just help himself to them.

Luckily the huge TV was on, to draw his attention away from the bed.

"*Carnal Knowledge!*" Neal said. "Lookit how young Jack Nicholson is! I saw this on Flix, did you?"

"Yeah. Nicholson's this college guy who says, 'She can put her shoes under my bed any day.'"

"That's it."

Big sets are hard to stop watching. I was able to smuggle everything past him and return it to the cabinet in the bathroom.

I hadn't slept a wink.

The main street in Serenity wasn't swept yet, and there were signs of the New Year's Eve celebrations, paper hats in the gutter and confetti ground into the slush that had been last night's snow.

Neal looked a little leftover, too, in his light-blue uniform jacket with the gold braid, and the black pants with the red stripe. The black officer's cap was pushed back on his head, his black hair mussed from his hand passing across it.

"Where did you finally end up sleeping?" I asked him.

"I told you I didn't sleep. I was sacked out in the solarium, watching the kilifish. I kept thinking of my father. He had an aquarium in the store, do you remember that?"

"Sure. And he'd hand out root beer barrels to kids."

"He would have liked to be a doctor. But Granddad Kraft was hard on him. He'd always tell him he was aiming too high. How's that for parental advice?"

I turned down Tal Bachman on the radio.

Neal said, "All night I kept thinking about back when we'd come here and I'd play pool with Dad and Mr. Evans. . . . Everything was so different then. It's hard to believe what can happen. You know, E.C.?"

"I know," I said. I really knew after a night of reading Rose Fitch's diaries.

Then, quickly, he changed the subject, the way he always did when he mentioned his father. "It was fun to be there for New Year's. She's fun. She's game for anything, isn't she?" He didn't wait for my answer. "Too bad she's not my type."

"You keep saying she's not your type," I said.

"She's not, E.C. I love that quirky, curious mind of hers, but you don't make love to a mind, you know? You don't hold someone in your arms and whisper, 'Tell me again how Kate Campbell came to write 'Signs Following.'"

"Neal, how do you think *she* feels?"

"I think she likes me."

"She's falling for you! She's really just a kid, too."

"So are you. What am I doing hanging out with kids!" He lit up a bidi. "What are you so excited about, anyway? What if I *did* like her that way, what of it?" He laughed and took one hand off the wheel to muss my hair. "Happy New Year! What are your resolutions?"

"One is to find out why you decided to be Richard Bachman on Christmas Eve."

"Yeah, I knew you were going to get around to that," he said. "You know how Mrs. Slaymaster has squeezed us for years. Kraft Drugs, Top Hat before it was KDS—that whole circle of stores behind the A&P. Some say she's greedy, but Mother says it's not that—it's her revenge on certain people in the town, my mother included."

I wondered how much Neal knew. I asked him why Rosalind Slaymaster would want to get even with his mother.

"Supposedly Mrs. Slaymaster was in love with my father." Neal looked embarrassed, as though it was as far-fetched as it sounded. "I don't think Mom even knows what's true and what isn't, anymore."

I could understand why he didn't believe his mother's version of the past. If I hadn't read the diary, I know I wouldn't have relied on Mrs. Kraft's scenario either. She was too edgy.

Neal shrugged. "I just didn't want Mrs. Slaymaster to know a Kraft would go to one of her parties. I went up there late and avoided meeting her, but I *had* to sign the guest book. Soooo—I often use that disguise."

"But your mother was *there*."

"Mrs. Slaymaster wouldn't know Mother if she fell over her. Mom sees her around town a lot, and there's not a flicker of recognition."

"Since we're on the subject of that party," I said, "are you planning to return the lighter *and* the cigarette case?"

Neal let out a long-suffering sigh. "I'm taking both things back, so relax! I don't want anything from Peligro!"

"Then why did you swipe stuff?"

"To get away with it. You don't understand. You don't have a game in you!" He sucked on the bidi. "Julie does," he said. "That's what I like about her."

166

I asked him to stop a few doors from the house. I didn't think Mom, The Duck, or my aunt heard me come in.

Somehow Doon always knew when it was me. He didn't let out a peep. He'd been waiting up for me.

Cats have other ideas. Any port in a storm, any round belly under the covers. Arbus, the traitor, was in my room with Darwin Duke.

Or so I thought.

When I tiptoed in to get my jeans, I saw Aunt Sheila in my bed with Arbus wrapped around her neck like a fur stole.

I had half an hour to sneak a nap in, but I couldn't sleep.

I tried to mull over everything I'd read in the scrapbook and the diaries, but I kept thinking of The Duck down the hall, in bed with my mother. The time I had before leaving for work I spent sacked out on the living-room floor with Doon. I let him lick my face. When he did, his tail pounded the floor in ecstasy.

Dad always used to make breakfast on New Year's Day.

After I finished wrapping the newspapers, I planned to go home and scramble some eggs for Mom and Aunt Sheila. I was sure the doctor wouldn't hang around. I had purposely left the shoes I'd worn the night before in the living room, along with a new sweater Mom had given me. So The Duck by then had the message that I'd dropped by in the early hours of the morning, and that I knew where *he'd* "bunked," as he'd put it. I believed he would have the decency to get out of there.

But right in front of our house sat the Saab. Aunt Sheila's Ford was gone.

Doctor Duke greeted me at the door with an apron on. He wanted to know what kind of omelet he could whip up for me.

"Your mother tells me your dad was quite a good short-order cook," he said. "I'm not in his class, probably, but now that he's gone, I'm willing to give it a try."

I hated him for appearing in our kitchen after he'd slept over, like he was entitled . . . like he was suddenly part of the family.

And I didn't like anyone saying Dad was gone, or that we'd lost him, as though he'd just stepped out of our lives for a while, or as though he'd gone to the mall with us and disappeared somewhere in the Gap.

What right did Darwin Duke have putting on an apron and horning in on something he didn't have anything to do with?

Even though I was hungry, I thanked The Duck just the same and went to bed.

When I woke up, I found Mom's note telling me she was going to an auction in Lambertville with "persistent Aries," as she sometimes called Duke. She would be back to make us ("just us") fresh pork with sauerkraut for dinner. Then shoofly pie. Dad's favorites.

Eighteen

Because Julie had forgotten to pack Peale's orange jacket, we were just off the main kitchen at Peligro, in The Package Room.

It was called that because its only purpose was to have packages wrapped in it, some for presenting as gifts, some for mailing, or both.

There were spools of ribbons, all sizes, textures, and colors, and rolls of paper, plain or decorated for birthdays, holidays, any occasion you could dream up. Name it and there it was. Tie it up, then pick out an appropriate card from the rack on the wall.

Just another little convenience in Peligroland!

"What's so important about Peale getting that jacket?"

"He has to have his blazer to go hunting," Julie said. "He's going on a hunt with Aunt Rosalind in San Antonio."

She was cutting tape and wrapping it around the package.

"All of her hunting crowd think Peale brings luck."

"Do you?"

"A lot of people do, but I'm not sure. See, Aunt claims Peale told her to adopt me. Now, was that my lucky day or my unlucky day? I might have been adopted by someone sane and had real siblings instead of The Leatherman."

Two, sometimes three afternoons a week Neal taught at KDS. When he could, he'd join us. But most afternoons after school just Julie and I headed for Peligro. When the weather was bad, Frazier would drive the Hummer to school and pick us up.

"Neal e-mailed me that he quit group. Did he tell you?"

"Did he say why?"

"He says he doesn't trust Wo-o-o Feelings anymore, particularly since he's so stuck on Aunt! I told Neal how he calls her every day. He sent her another flowering tree, too. Aunt said it's a gardenia bush. We don't have anything like that growing on the ranch. Aunt loves to get presents, particularly when they cost money. She practically never does, unless it's one of Simon Slaymaster's poor relatives sucking up to her on her birthday."

"That's pretty serious: Neal quitting group. He needs it."

"He knows he needs it. But *Aunt* doesn't need to discover I'm hanging out with the mysterious Richard Bachman, does she?"

"So he confessed, did he?"

"In e-mail, the coward! He was afraid I'd dump him."

"Is that what he said?"

"He said he didn't blame me if I dumped him."

"That sounds like the two of you are going together."

"No, the three of us are. Haven't you heard there's safety in numbers?"

"I don't know why he pulls stuff like that."

"Because he's dark and deep," Julie said.

"Is that what he is?"

Every day I was with her there, I planned to bring up the diaries and the scrapbook. I wondered if she knew they were there, and if she'd read them. I wasn't at all sure she had. She hadn't lived at Peligro long enough to know what was in every room.

But something stopped me from talking about it. Not "something." *Neal.* I just didn't want to confess I'd gone through Mrs. Slaymaster's personal papers, on top of Neal walking off with the silver. It sounded too much like The Invasion of the Private Property Snatchers. I decided I'd wait for the right time to bring it up. I saw us talking about it on a summer day.

Julie tried to get interested in other Stephen King movies after *Carrie.* Neal often brought one with him, and always he brought new CDs, great, hot music that filled every room. We always had music on, with or without Neal. Peligro seemed to be set to music.

When Neal wasn't with us, Julie and I watched old Carson McCullers movies—her favorites. I liked them, too. That afternoon after she finished getting Peale's jacket ready to mail, we watched *The Member of the Wedding*. Julie said five years ago she was just like Frankie, "'this unjoined person,'" she quoted, "'who hung around in the doorways and was afraid.'

"I love that line!" she said. "Neal says McCullers is too into losers for him."

"Yeah," I said. "Neal the winner."

No matter what we were talking about, the subject always came back to Neal. I suppose I envied him for that, or resented him because of it. I don't think I was aware of any feelings like that at the time, but how could I not have? How had I kept myself from telling Julie she really didn't know him? From saying, "Maybe if you knew him, you wouldn't be so gaga over him."

Julie asked me to blow up one of the New Year's Eve photos of Neal. He was bare chested, in his trunks, wearing the cone-shaped paper hat, standing at the stove scrambling eggs, in profile, with the bidi hanging from his lips. She was going to keep it in her underwear drawer. "No smart remarks," she said to me.

She had copies of all the photos I'd taken New Year's Eve. In one she and Neal were mooning the camera, and in another all three of us stood there bare assed, our backs turned to the camera. I'd set a timer to take it.

"I wish we could stay in this month for a year," Julie said.

"If you're going to wish for a month, wish for a warm one."

"It isn't the weather. It's the way we are *right now*. It's us after school, and it's the way I look forward to seeing Neal when he comes. I'm never disappointed." She reached out and touched my sleeve. "I love the two of you."

"I know. In different ways."

"Yes. But you're part of us."

They would beg me to stay times I wanted to give them a chance to be alone. It was almost as though they were afraid of what could happen if I left—not afraid of falling into each other's arms, I didn't think, but afraid of not falling into each other's arms. Afraid of one-on-one. I knew what it was like from days when I first fell for Arden Cutler. At first we'd hung out in a gang. It was a while and some trembling time in the backseat of a Honda with the front seat taken, too, before we were okay alone together.

But Neal was older. Neal was used to girls from being around them at KDS. I couldn't figure Neal out.

"Right now I'd rather be with her than anyone," he told me once as we were driving away from Peligro. "But I don't understand myself."

"What's to understand? You really like her, but you don't love her. Why do you theorize so much?"

"Why don't you *ever* theorize?"

"I theorize plenty!"

"Then why isn't there something between like and love?"

That stopped me.

"Something more than like but less than love," he insisted.

"Good question, Neal," I said, because I didn't have an answer to that one.

Mrs. Rosenkrantz, the housekeeper, rarely left her third-floor apartment, where her afternoons were spent with soaps and talk shows. When Julie and I would arrive at Peligro after school, only Bob was there to greet us, tossing a rubber bone in the air and charging at it, a dachshund hint that a romp was due.

Sometimes we would hear a squeak on the back stairs and we'd know Mrs. Rosenkrantz had ventured down for something but turned back when she heard our voices. Or maybe, as *I* imagined, she really was spying on us. A few times when we were out in the yard, I would see the curtains in her bedroom move, as though she was right behind them.

One night when I got home, Doctor Duke was sitting on our living-room couch, waiting for Mom to finish dressing. They were going across the bridge to have dinner with Aunt

Sheila and a massage therapist she'd started dating.

I hadn't mentioned the gardenia tree or the orchid tree to my mother. I'd come close, but she was in such a good mood lately, I didn't want to spoil it.

I kept telling myself to remember what I'd thought of the doctor when I first knew him.

What came to mind most often was what he'd said about weeping with one eye.

I'd brought in some photographs Dad had taken of a canned hunt in the next county. It was run by this guy who advertised "If You Don't Make a Kill, You Don't get a Bill!" He'd stocked fifty acres of fenced-in land with old animals from zoos, or sick ones, or ones that had been used in experiments. Easy kills.

"I couldn't take pictures like that," I'd told the doctor. "I'd get too angry, or too sick to my stomach. That's the difference between Dad and me. I don't know how he did it."

"I do," Duke had said. "You develop a talent for weeping with one eye. War correspondents have it, photojournalists, clergypeople, therapists, writers. You keep one eye alert and unsentimental."

Could the same man who said that to me, and sounded so wise, be this dip leaning forward on our couch to pick out all the candy with soft centers in a box of Fanny Farmers?

He was wearing some sickly-sweet aftershave. He smelled like Peale.

"How's everything going, E.C.?"

"Fine."

"Your mother tells me you spend a lot of time at Peligro."

"Uh-huh."

"You and Neal."

A little fishing expedition, I figured. I didn't answer him. I hung my coat up and tossed a copy of *The Heart Is a Lonely Hunter* on the table. It was the Carson McCullers novel I'd promised Julie I'd read before we watched the movie. The movie was over thirty years old, but Julie said it was the best thing Alan Arkin ever made.

"E.C.?" said The Duck. "I just want to say one thing."

"Go ahead," I said. Arbus was rubbing one side of her face against my Dockers.

"I hope that you and Neal appreciate the fact that this is a young woman who has had very little exposure to boys."

"I know that," I said. "Excuse me. I have to feed the animals."

"I'm sorry, E.C., that you're so very closed to having some sort of rapport with me."

Mom came down the staircase at that point, relieving me of having to answer The Duck.

"Darwin? Who's this stranger?" she said. "Anyone we know?"

"You'll have to ask him," The Duck grumbled, and unwrapped the last chocolate cherry in the box.

"We haven't seen much of you, honey," Mom said.

"I'm around."

"I know *that*. But I'm afraid we've lost you to Peligro." She went across to the closet as The Duck popped the chocolate cherry into his mouth. Then he scrambled across to help Mom on with her coat.

I told them good night and went into the kitchen.

In a moment Mom appeared in the doorway. "E.C.?" she said. "I'm a little concerned about your latest photos. They've been sitting out on your desk for days now. I couldn't help but see them."

"We were swimming, Mom."

"I realize that. . . . I just don't think it's appropriate to take pictures like that. You and Neal can do what you like together, but where Julie's concerned, please use more judgment."

"All right."

I suddenly knew how Quack Quack had come up with the word "exposure."

One thing I hated was her talking about me, my life, with *him*, the same as she might have talked with Dad.

What if she marries him? I thought. I opened a can of mackerel and had an odor to go with the image.

I always like watching the animals eat. Doon dove into his Alpo nose first, and it was finished before a slow count to ten. Arbus, on the nine count, was just making up her mind

177

to have a whiff of the evening's fare. Mackerel was her favorite. But her faithful servant (Edgar C. Tobbit) would be the last to know. She was enjoying a leisurely stroll from the kitchen back to the living room, her tail flagging smartly. Perhaps a little couch clawing before dinner, to work up an appetite.

"Who cares if you don't eat, Arbus?" I said.

Arbus knew darn well who cared.

I heard the Saab leave the driveway, and just as I was washing the fishy smell from my hands, Neal called.

"Can I come over right now?" he said.

"Sure, but what's the matter?"

"*Everything.* Okay?"

Nineteen

"Wait till you see this," Neal said, handing me a white envelope. "Mrs. Slaymaster had Frazier drive the Hummer down to KDS and drop it off. Luckily I was having a smoke outside, and Mom was in with a toe/tap class."

"Mrs. Slaymaster's not at Peligro. I was just there."

"She's not at Peligro *yet*," Neal said. "Look at this! She must have had these all printed up, waiting to hand out after big parties!"

He passed me an envelope. I took out a piece of thick white paper with a white S embossed on the top.

In the center, handwritten, was:

One sterling silver cigarette lighter....................$400.00
One sterling silver cigarette case *$1000.00*
Total debt...$1400.00

Underneath that in raised print:

> *Our security camera photographed your theft of*
> *this. A member of the police department identified*
> *you. Return the property or be prepared to face the*
> *consequences.*

That part was crossed out. Underneath, part of a fax was pasted to the stationery.

> *Dear Mr. Bachman/Kraft,*
>
> *I am contemplating pressing charges, not just for*
> *your theft of these articles, but for other things such*
> *as masquerading under a false identity while you*
> *helped yourself.*
>
> *Be at Peligro at 5 P.M. tomorrow and we will*
> *discuss this. Please ask your mother to accompany*
> *you. Rosalind Slaymaster.*

"How did she find out you're Bachman?"

Neal was trying to keep a bidi lit. He said, "Diego's the one who took everyone's name, the one with the photographic memory. He must have taken the film to the police and asked them about Bachman. One of the cops said, '*Bachman?* That's Neal Kraft.' . . . Right?"

"It sounds logical."

"Julie told me once that her aunt was trying to get the names of all the Don't Ditch Dutchman people. *They* were all photographed too, I suppose, blowing up balloons, writing on bathroom walls, pasting stickers to tables. She wants to keep track of them."

"And you."

"She wants to ruin *me*, E.C." Neal slumped down in the kitchen chair.

"She can't ruin you, Neal. She can make things uncomfortable for you but not ruin you."

"*Ruin* me. You don't know."

"Oh, come on, Neal!"

"It's serious, E.C. Now the police know."

"She says she's *contemplating* pressing charges. If you return the things, she'll probably just bawl you out. . . . Anyway, It's your first offense."

"No, it isn't."

I looked at him.

He said, "I've been picked up two times for shoplifting."

"*When?*"

"Last fall."

"Where? How?"

"Once at the Gap. I was walking off wearing a coat. And once I was getting some scarves for our Easter recital at Saks Fifth Avenue over in Lambertville. . . . They don't let you go, you know. It's mall policy to apprehend shoplifters."

There wasn't any point in asking him why he did it then, why he took such a chance. I don't think he knew himself.

"Have you told your mother?" I asked him.

"Hell, no! My mother? My mother will kill me!"

"Let's call Julie," I said.

"She's not taking calls this evening, according to Mrs. Rosenkrantz. She's *awaiting* the arrival of her aunt! I sent her e-mail, but . . ." He threw his hands up.

"And Mrs. Slaymaster is on her way home because of this?"

"I don't *know* why she's on her way home!"

"Are you going to Peligro with your mother?"

"No way!"

"But you're going to be there, right? You're going to return her stuff?"

"My gawd, E.C. Let up! You're obsessed with me returning her shit!"

"If you want to see Julie again, you'd better."

Neal shook his head mournfully. "Mrs. Slaymaster's going to put my ass in the slammer, E.C.! I fell into her lap like a gift from heaven! I told you she's always had it in for us Krafts! You probably don't believe it."

I wondered again if it would help anything if I told him about what I'd read in the diaries. I knew better. I knew Neal. He'd only obsess about getting his hands on them.

"I believe it," I said.

"Of all people to steal from! A lady with a SecureUSystem."

"You'd probably be safer not stealing from anyone," I said.

"Wise guy," he said.

We went into the living room and looked for e-mail, but there wasn't any.

"What am I going to do?" Neal asked me.

I didn't know. It was like the time I had no answer when he'd wanted to know if there was something between like and love.

Twenty

I went to school way ahead of time, then waited about half an hour for the Hummer to come rumbling down the street.

Mrs. Slaymaster was behind the wheel.

I knew Julie saw me wave, but she didn't wave back as she came down the walk toward me.

Her face was grim, and she was shaking her head.

"Where's Neal, Eddie? Do you know?"

"He said he was skipping school today. He wanted time to think."

"He better not skip the meeting with Aunt. You know about it, don't you?"

"Yeah, he showed me those engraved cards telling the recipients they were caught stealing. Where'd she get that idea?"

"It started in Texas, when she was adding stables and the workers were walking off with everything. She never used them for *parties* there. . . . Oh, Eddie, everything's become so awful."

"Tell me what's going on."

"Aunt's forbidden me to see Neal, speak with him, e-mail him. She'd forbid me to think about him if there was any way she could."

We were standing in everyone's way, in the center of the sidewalk. I led Julie over to the side.

I said, "First let me get something straight. Diego just routinely went to the police with the party film? Is that how this came about?"

"It's more complicated. . . . Don't feel badly, Eddie, because none of this is your fault. But somehow Mrs. Rosenkrantz found those photographs you took New Year's Eve. . . . All the time I thought she never left her apartment, she must have been snooping in my room."

"Has your aunt seen them?"

"They were sent to her by overnight mail."

I hit my head with my palm. "Damn!"

Julie put her hand on my arm. "I haven't told you the worst news."

We stood on the grass by the front entrance, snow starting to fall. We could see our breath as we talked.

"Aunt's taking me to Texas tomorrow. She says she's enrolling me in a boarding school near Ingram. Then she's going to see about sending me to Le Rosey."

"What's that mean?" Even as I asked the question, I remembered Rose Fitch asking it, too, at the Garden Party. I remembered she'd described how Neal's father had laughed, as though she'd made a joke.

"It's this posh prep school in Switzerland," Julie said, "Institut le Rosey. It was her second choice after Chalfont."

"Is she *serious*, Julie?" When wasn't Rosalind Slaymaster serious?

"Dead serious! She's been getting some threatening mail, too, from the Dutchman Park protesters. She says coming back here didn't work out."

"Does she mean it?"

"Paulo and Diego are going to take turns driving the Hummer, and she's giving Frazier notice. She's taking the Hummer, so she isn't planning to come back."

"After all the work she's put in up there?"

"That's the way Aunt is. If something doesn't pan out, she won't waste time ending it. She told me to clean out my locker and say my good-byes."

I just stood there in the cold.

"I don't want to go, Eddie."

"I know. I don't want you to go either."

"Maybe I should make an appointment with the dude with the scythe."

"Don't say that, Julie."

"I think of it a lot. Every time we head for that ranch, I think of it!"

The school bell rang.

I opened the door for us.

"She wants to see you, Eddie."

"What for?"

"She said she wants to close the account."

"What does that mean?"

"I don't know. I wish *you* could change her mind."

"*Me* change *her* mind?"

"Or do something. She was on the horn at quarter to eight this morning, fighting with the contractor, then leaving messages on answering machines for the local realtors. Peligro's going on the market."

"How can she—"

"She can," Julie said. "I think this town has always been her nemesis. . . . Frazier's coming for me after school. She said to ride back with us."

"What do you think I should do?"

"It might be our last time together."

"It won't be." I didn't know how to let go of the idea I could protect her. "I'll go back with you, though," I said.

"What do you mean it won't be?"

"I mean not to worry," I told her.

I wondered if my words sounded as unconvincing to Julie as they did to me.

Twenty-one

Rosalind Slaymaster was sitting in the kitchen, at the white table, watching the stock-market reports on CNBC. Beside her sat Peale in loafers, jeans, a white shirt, and a green V-neck sweater.

She stood up as we came through the door. She, too, was in jeans, a green V-neck sweater, and a white shirt.

"Hello, Mrs. Slaymaster," I said.

She acted as though I hadn't spoken and wasn't there.

"Julie, I want you to go down to the Parlas' and see if Diego knows where your steamer trunk is."

"Yes, ma'am."

"Tell Paulo the contractor is coming by at four thirty for his pay, and I want Paulo beside me should there be any nastiness."

"Yes, ma'am."

When Julie left, she deigned to notice me. "Follow me, Tobbit."

She led the way. I followed. Bob the dachshund waddled along behind me.

In the living room she sat in this white chair in front of a wall of bookcases. There was a tall ladder on wheels leaning into the books.

Mrs. Slaymaster motioned for me to take the other white chair, not far from hers.

Then she surprised me by pulling a pack of Marlboros from her shirt pocket, shaking one up, and lighting it.

I'd never seen her smoke before.

As though she could read my mind, she said, "This is your fault, Tobbit," holding up the cigarette caught between her large, long fingers. "I haven't smoked since Peale came into my life. I didn't want him smelling of tobacco."

"Okay."

"In fact, Edgar Cayce Tobbit, this entire mess is your fault! I first invited you here under the pretense I wanted your mother to do Peale's horoscope. Why would I let your mother do something for Peale that I trust only Sandra Cole to do for Julie and me?"

I didn't have an answer for that one, so I watched her suck on the cigarette and hoped the scientists were right about nicotine killing people.

She said, "I wanted Julie to have someone on her side. I never had anyone on my side when I went to that high school, but I've got a tougher hide! Julie doesn't relate well to other girls. So I called on Doctor Duke." Another long drag. She was the kind of smoker who talked while the smoke was still exiting her lungs. "I found out that he was the SHS counselor, something we didn't have in my day, and survived without, thank you very much. I phoned him and asked him to find me someone to befriend Julie."

"Did she ever know that?"

"Of course not! She'd never be friends with anyone I'd set up for that purpose! Don't you know *anything* about her by now?"

Another drag.

"Darwin Duke told me your father died and you were having a hard time handling it," she said. "He told me you'd also just broken up with some girl. Said you were quiet, interested in photography and writing, not a rah-rah jock or a troublemaker. That sounded good to me." She shook her head. "We all make mistakes."

"You may have set it up, Mrs. Slaymaster," I said, "but I'm Julie's true friend,"

"Really?" A long stream of smoke exhaled.

"I would do anything for her."

"Good. There's something you can do for her right away.

191

Leave her alone. My niece does not need the kind of friend who won't stand with her when a group of silly schoolgirls play a mean trick on her! You walked out like the coward you are."

"Mrs. Slaymaster," I said between my teeth, "can't you let go of anything? Do you know how many times you've brought that up?"

"Be quiet! I haven't finished!"

I stared down at the thick rug under my feet.

"Look at me!" she said.

I looked up at those cold, ice-green eyes, which narrowed as she focused on me. "You made a deal with me, Tobbit, to watch out for Julie. We shook on it. The next thing I know, you'd brought your scumbag friend into my house while I was away. The next thing I know, you took obscene photographs of Julie with that scumbag, and then lo and behold, the little coward behind the lens steps out and I am treated to the behinds of all three of you."

"I wasn't planning on treating *you* to our behinds," I said.

"Damn tooting you weren't! I don't know what other slimy action there was in my house while I was gone, but you are on my shit list *big*, Tobbit! I've already told your mother what a little sneaky creep she has on her hands!"

I stood up. "You're putting your own spin on something that wasn't like that at all!"

"Sit down, you yellowbelly!"

I didn't do it.

She stood up too. She was one of the few people I knew who were taller than I was. I *had* to look up to her.

"In twenty-four hours, Two-Bit, Julie, Peale, and I will be headed for Texas, for good!"

"I wish you wouldn't take Julie away. She was just beginning to—"

"To *what*? No one likes her here! She has no friends but you and your lowlife buddy. I know that family, those Krafts. That filthy little thief. He comes here under a false name and walks away with the silver! Is that the kind of person you thought my niece should have as a friend? Someone who taught her to smoke filthy little cigarettes from India!"

She reached down and ground out her Marlboro, like it was my neck she was twisting with one hand. Then she looked at her watch and said she was expecting her contractor, as well as my riffraff friend and his mother, so I was to clear out.

"I also told your mother that if you come near Peligro or try to see, phone, or e-mail Julie, I'll go to the police and have a protection order drawn up. This is the last time you'll be on my property, and you have already seen Julie for the last time. Now leave the way you came, out the back!"

I was shaking, with anger and angst. I could feel her eyes following me down the hall. Bob, the dachshund, sneaked out with me, his tail between his legs as I headed for the kitchen.

There was a fellow just arriving, with two others behind him.

I figured they were probably part of the crew building the stables.

"Is the missus in?" he asked me.

I nodded, and he shouted, "Mrs. Slaymaster? It's Ernie Leogrande! I've got Tom and Karl here!"

"Come on down," she called back.

I looked across the kitchen and saw Peale. I could have sworn he was looking out at the bird feeder when I'd arrived, but at that moment his green eyes were fixed on me.

I gave him a little two-finger farewell salute.

"So long, take care," I said, realizing I'd never be able to say even that much to Julie.

I'd told her not to worry, as though I'd handle every-thing, as though suddenly I'd become a match for Rosalind Slaymaster.

I stood there feeling sad and helpless, bending over to pet Bob and calm him down after the tirade he'd heard from under a chair.

The thought came to me then that Mrs. Slaymaster never traveled without Peale.

There was a way, after all, that I could keep Julie from leaving Serenity. All I had to do was take Peale.

Twenty-Two

I fixed a place way back in my closet for Peale. I put him on a little stool and pushed my clothes down to the center, so he'd have breathing room. No one had ever proven to me Peale didn't breathe.

My mother never went into my closet. But never say never. I removed Peale's sweater, which reeked of Tommy, took it to the cellar, and tucked it inside a rolled-up rug.

I made a ransom note by cutting letters from magazines and newspapers. I copied the wording from a mystery novel, hoping that the idea of asking for $100,000 in unmarked bills out of sequence would give the demand a serious, authentic voice. A kidnaper who knew what he was doing. *Stand by,* I advised, *and I will be in touch with you about the particulars.*

The police arrived early that evening while my mother

was at her yoga class. Mrs. Slaymaster's conviction that I lived vicariously, on the sidelines of life, worked in my favor. They questioned me with smiles on their faces, petting Doon and chuckling at Arbus' antics as she skedaddled up the drapes, back down, then on a tear to the bedrooms. Her best performances were spontaneous ones for strangers.

The police were trying to find out exactly *when* Peale was taken. Had I seen him when I left the kitchen at Peligro?

The prime suspects were the ones whose appointments came after mine that afternoon: the contractors, who had just been fired, ditto the electrician, and Neal, who had left Peligro with the news that Mrs. Slaymaster was going to press charges for the theft of her silver cigarette case and lighter. There had also been a handful of Dutchman protesters down on the road. But I heard Officer Klaich comment that it could have been anyone in town, since "Rosie" wasn't known for the number of people who wished her well.

Nevertheless, the dollnaping was being taken very seriously. The police might call her "Rosie" with their lips sliding into smiles, but not a one of them wanted any trouble with Rosalind Slaymaster. She was too powerful and too vengeful.

Although the consensus was that Neal was the culprit, an investigation was under way. Neal was being held at the Serenity jail for theft of property—not just the cigarette case and the lighter, but add the suspicion he had taken Peale to the list as well. It was up to a judge to review the evidence and fix bail.

I decided to move Peale as soon as I had a chance. Cover him carefully and put him in the ground.

When Mom got home that night, she came into my room shaking her head from side to side. "You're certainly out of favor up Peligro way."

"She's blown it all out of proportion—" I started to defend myself, but Mom came over and smoothed my hair back with her hand.

"Honey, I know. . . . I'm sorry. I'm most sorry for Julie."

"Did you hear that Peale was kidnaped?"

"I heard Neal took him."

"He didn't, though. He's in the slammer for it, but he didn't do it!"

"Darwin says that Neal's in jail because he stole silver from Peligro on Christmas Eve."

"But they'll hang Peale's kidnaping on him too."

"Did he take silver from Peligro, honey?"

"He doesn't take things so he can sell them or anything."

"But he took some things of value from the Christmas Eve party?"

"Yeah, he did."

"Are you sure he didn't take Peale too?"

"Mom, he'd just got caught taking the silver! Why would he take Peale?"

"Maybe to get even with her for catching him in the act on camera."

"Oh, Mom!"

"Well? Everyone in town says he took Peale."

"Then everyone in town is wrong!"

She gave me this look that said she wasn't so sure, but she didn't press the point.

I knew she wanted to be in a quiet mood for her nightly yoga.

Early the next morning, before I went down to wrap the out-of-town newspapers, I hiked up to Peligro and put the ransom note in the mailbox. It was still dark out.

Twenty-Three

I don't think any of us realized that Mrs. Slaymaster would be news outside of Serenity and Texas. Peale helped, of course. Instead of being simply the widow of the man who single-handedly invented the Fullflush instrument, which revolutionized oil services and made him worth billions, she became the "eccentric" widow. The victim of a dollnaping!

AP and UPI camerapeople were shooting pictures of Peligro, Serenity High School, the white Hummer, Kraft Dance Studios ("a possible suspect is an instructor here"), even the poster offering:

$10,000 REWARD

One morning my old nemesis, Arden, deigned to communicate with me long enough to say excitedly that *60 Minutes* was coming to interview some of The Sluts who knew Neal and Julie and me.

"Who would *they* be?" I asked sarcastically.

"Oh, E.C. You're a party pooper. We all know you've been hanging out at Peligro, and the rumor is Neal was just casing Peligro. You knew Neal took stuff."

"No, I didn't." Was I the last to learn that?

"He took the doll, didn't he?"

"Like I'd tell *you*," I said.

"I'm glad you're still bitter," she informed me. "That means you really cared about me."

"How *I* felt about *you* was never the problem," I said.

It was the first one-on-one conversation we'd had since one of the dreary loved-you-but-didn't-like-you-but-wasn't-in-love et cetera chats. Nelson Marland stood nearby holding her coat, looking like just another fat kid, not the football hero we'd cheered for Saturday afternoons.

Julie wasn't allowed to return to school, since Mrs. Slaymaster claimed she was being transferred to one out of state. The only time I was ever able to talk with Julie was when she called me. I knew that someone was monitoring the call. She telephoned a few times, begging me to tell her anything I knew or heard about Peale's "abduction." I knew that word wasn't hers. That word was from the same vocabulary as "perpetrator," "apprehend," and "remand." She never called me Eddie, either. I knew she had company.

No e-mail was coming through, except the kind with stiff wording, similar to the tense pleas Julie made over the telephone. The please, please, please, if you know who has Peale, help us get him back kind.

I wondered if she remembered that morning at SHS when she'd asked me to do something, and I'd said not to worry.

I wanted to believe that somehow she knew I had Peale, and that I had taken him to keep her in Serenity. Then she would guess that no harm would come to Peale, and that there was nothing to fear from some disgruntled crank.

What I hoped for was that gradually Mrs. Slaymaster would accept that Peale was gone but stay in Serenity, the way parents of missing children often refused to move. My father had done a story about it once. Many parents felt somehow their kids would find their way back if they stayed put.

Neal was being held without bail. The judge said it looked as though he hadn't learned from his two other arrests.

I believed that the only reason the police allowed me to visit him was that they'd wired the reception area hoping we'd say something incriminating.

The Serenity police were hot after a solution, since Mrs. Slaymaster could conceivably make a contribution to their building fund. They might have to name all the jail cells after her, but not many locals had sentimental feelings about them anyway.

I asked Neal, "Who do *you* think took Peale?" I was curious to know what he'd say.

"I haven't a clue, because there're so many possibilities. Start with the Don't Ditch Dutchman crowd. . . . Next, her workers—she always treated them like shit! . . . Or it could be some tenant whose rent she raised recently. I even wondered if it was my mother, at one point. Or *you*." He grinned. "Maybe some of me rubbed off on you, buddy!"

"Maybe."

"How's Julie doing?"

"I wouldn't know."

"Isn't there any way you can get through to her?"

"No."

"What the hell are we going to do, just let her go?"

"Neal," I said, "Mrs. Slaymaster won't leave here without Peale."

He looked at me.

He said, "You're right. . . . Why didn't *I* think of that?"

"The best thinking isn't done in a jail cell," I said.

Neal had that same half smile on his face that always told you he wasn't going under. He was resilient, no matter what.

He gave me the name of a guy in his class he thought

would make copies of his homework assignments, and he asked me to check on his mom, make sure things were okay at KDS.

All the while I spoke with Neal's mother, I couldn't forget the Shirley Bryan of Rose's diary. Couldn't quite believe it, either. I'd seen her mad, as she was that afternoon, plenty of times, but I'd never seen her mean.

I wondered—if someone was keeping a diary about me, would I be recognizable to others years away?

Mrs. Kraft had black hair that afternoon. She changed hair color the same way Neal changed what he wore.

"I blame this on you," she said, exactly as Mrs. Slaymaster had. She was in a tutu with a man's long white shirt over it, a red ribbon holding her shoulder-length hair back. She was a scowling Kewpie doll. "You got Cornelius to go up there in the first place," she accused.

Neal always became Cornelius in stressful times.

"I'm sorry, Mrs. Kraft. I just invited him to a party."

"You didn't know the can of worms you were opening. . . . Neal used to go there with his father when he was a kid. I think he got his taste for luxury up at Evans Above. He'd come home and he'd say why can't we have heated towel racks? So I'd say of course, that's what we need—you hit the nail on the head! We don't have a thousand dollars saved toward your college, but we need the towel racks heated. . . . You know he's been stealing from stores?"

"Yes, ma'am."

"I didn't know Rose Slaymaster asked me to accompany him when she saw him, or I would have gone up there and given her a piece of my mind! Imagine! Giving a party, then photographing the guests to see who'd steal!"

"She caught the Butler sisters too."

"That's not news, that those two filch things. . . . I blame this Julie Slaymaster, too!" said Mrs. Kraft. "She should have warned Neal there was a camera."

"She probably never dreamed he'd take stuff. . . . I didn't either."

"Dr. Duke says it's symbolic. A desperate effort to recover loss. Apparently it's all tied in with my husband's suicide."

"I don't know, ma'am."

"Of course you don't know!" she said in her furious tones.

Before I left, she looked up at me with her head cocked to one side and said, "Where did he put Peale, E.C.?"

"He didn't take him, ma'am."

"I'd like to believe that," she said in a disbelieving tone.

Meanwhile, the weather had turned mild, almost like having an Indian summer in the middle of February. It made me think of possibly digging up the ground behind our garage and finding something waterproof to wrap Peale in.

Mrs. Slaymaster was now urging the kidnaper to contact her. She took full-page ads in the newspaper and printed posters that were distributed throughout Serenity. In my ransom note I had said I would call soon announcing the amount of money I wanted. *Stand by for the particulars.* Mrs. Slaymaster begged "whoever you may be" to get in touch with her immediately. Everyone was laughing about it, because she was appealing to the kidnaper's "sense of fairness," as though someone like her would know what that even meant.

The unexpectedly warm weather seemed to heat up The Duck, for he began calling my mother, while she made excuses for why she couldn't have dinner with him. She was making him pay, I supposed, for spending so much time at Peligro, neglecting her while he helped Mrs. Slaymaster through the crisis.

Finally he put the invitation another way: He needed advice about Neal and Julie and Mrs. Slaymaster. He wanted me to come along.

"Where would we eat?" I asked Mom.

"He said The Canal House." Mom laughed. "Then he said 'my treat,' as though that was a big deal! Did I tell you that I called off our Saint Martin trip?"

"No. Why?"

"He kept calling it our Valentine trip. Then the other night he said he'd pay for the room and meals, but I'd have to split the airfare with him and what it'd cost to rent a car."

I had nothing to say. My mind was stopped on the word "room," singular.

"Can you believe it?" Mom said. "Darwin makes five times what I do, and he has no dependents . . . no one to put through college."

I knew it was an appropriate time to mention orchid and gardenia trees, but Mom's laughter wasn't the kind she was enjoying, I could tell.

It was survival laughter: If I don't laugh, I'll bawl.

I said, "Mom, I know the shortage of males in Bucks County is beyond disaster, but how can you—"

She shushed me with one finger held up to my lips.

"People have flaws, E.C.; even loved ones do."

"Is that what you think of him as—a loved one?" I said.

Mom said, "Give him a break, honey."

So she did.

Twenty-four

Dinner at The Canal House.

"My treat!" the doctor announced grandly, up on tiptoe to sling his arm around my shoulders. "I'm delighted you accepted my invitation to join us, Edgar."

Even though the weather was unusual for February, we were the only ones in an open convertible. The Duck drove top down any chance he got. Sinatra sang at full volume, the doctor waving one hand in rhythm, coming on strong as he joined Ol' Blue Eyes questioning "What Is This Thing Called Love?"

Even though Mom was not a vegetarian, she ordered the vegetarian special because it was the cheapest dish on the menu. Wo-o-o Feelings had trained her well.

I ordered the large porterhouse.

"It's enormous, E.C.," said the doctor. "Are you sure

you don't want the New York cut?"

Mom got his cheap drift and said, "Maybe you'd better have the smaller size, sweetheart. You'll never finish a big one."

"Then I'll treat Doon."

The doctor winced.

"He *needs* a treat," said Mom. "I didn't have a chance to give him a long walk before we left. What a day I had!"

"So you really want the porterhouse?" the doctor asked as the waitress came for our order.

"I really do," I said.

"Suit yourself."

He ordered one for himself, too.

"How is Mrs. Slaymaster?" Mom asked immediately.

"I had Doctor Kamitses come over and give her a sedative this afternoon," he said. "She can't sleep. . . . The abduction of this doll sounds like a trivial thing, even a comic thing, but in Rosalind's life it's major—it's, in fact, horrendous!"

"I saw it coming," said my mother.

"How can you say you saw it coming?"

"I did Peale's horoscope. I saw peril in his future."

Doctor Duke made a face. "I don't mind indulging Rosalind on this issue, but I count on you, Ann, not to aggravate the absurdity of it all by pretending that inanimate things have astrological signs. Astrology is ridiculous enough!"

"Inanimate things *do* have signs. Why, even Philadelphia does," said my mother.

"Philadelphia does," the doctor said with the same tone of voice Mrs. S. used when she said, "Cow pie!"

"Its rising sign is Virgo and its sun sign is Cancer."

"What's the United States?" I asked, because I knew this subject drove The Duck up the wall. Fan the flames.

"Your sign, honey. Gemini."

The doctor took a gulp of his martini. His face was beet red.

"I think we won't discuss astrology anymore," said my mother.

"I think that's wise," he said. "We won't discuss astrology, reincarnation, divination, other-life experiences, or clairsentience."

"What's clairsentience?"

"Ask your mother!" the doctor barked.

"It's this feeling I've had all day," said my mother. "It's a feeling that something's going to happen."

"Something happens every day!" the doctor said.

"No, not something ordinary. I feel it's a presentiment of some kind."

"Pssssss. Presentiment," the doctor hissed.

"I just wish I knew Neptune's configuration right now. Neptune rules the psychic sense."

"Well, I rule the wine list," said the doctor. "I want to order a good bottle of wine for our dinner, Ann. My treat. I tasted an extraordinary Lynch-Bages at Peligro the other night, unfortunate because there was so much unhappiness at the table. . . . But you know, Rosalind is famous for her cellar."

"I didn't know," Mom said.

"Oh, yes, famous." He snapped his fingers for the maitre d'.

He said, "She's a little inexperienced when it comes to white wine, but I can help her out there."

As soon as our dinners were served, a large, noisy party arrived and sat down across the room.

When the proprietor came over to apologize for the noise, he informed us they were the crew from *Fast Copy*.

"Don't tell them about my connection to Rosalind Slaymaster," said the doctor.

"Of course not, Doctor Duke. I don't even know about that connection."

"I've been helping her deal with this crisis."

"The poor lady. Whenever she came here for lunch or dinner, she brought the toy with her. He sat right up at the table like a little person."

The *Fast Copy* crew was feeding the jukebox and beginning to dance in the center of the room.

"It's the girl I feel most sorry for," said the doctor after the proprietor wished us *bon appetit*. "Julie."

"What about Julie?" I asked him.

"Rosalind is a very perspicacious woman," said The

Duck, answering my question in one of his typical round-about ways. "Maybe she doesn't have my training, but her theories are interesting and often true. One of her theories is that a person involved in photography is more of a watcher than a doer."

"Edgar writes, too," said my mother.

"Mrs. Slaymaster believes that watchers need doers to do all the things they don't have the guts, cancel that—the *will* to do themselves."

"Like what?" I asked him.

"Let me finish. . . . And doers need watchers to impress."

"Just say what you mean, Darwin," said my mother.

"What I mean is that if there is any possibility that Neal Kraft knows where Peale is, and sees that Peale's returned, Mrs. Slaymaster will not press any charges. Neal will go back to his life, and she will return to hers on The Lucky Star."

"With Julie," I said.

"Of course with Julie. . . . But if Peale is returned safely, there's nothing preventing Julie from visiting. You could see her then. After a sufficient amount of time passes, *possibly* even Neal could see her as well. Peligro will be on the market for some time. And even if it isn't . . ." The doctor shrugged.

"Then Mrs. Slaymaster's changed her tune," I said. "Boy, has she!"

"We all change our tunes from time to time," he said.

"I didn't know *she* did," I said.

"Because you don't know her," he said. "You don't know what a truly lovely person Rosalind Slaymaster is."

The doctor took a long swallow of his Merlot. I gave Mom an eyes-to-ceiling look, and she grabbed her wine glass too.

The doctor resumed then, wiping his lips, slicing his steak. "I understand why Neal Kraft took Peale, if he did—giving him the benefit of the doubt—but I don't understand this supposed interest he has in Julie. There are police who theorize that Neal is keeping this doll because he knows it'll keep Rosalind in Serenity."

"Why would Neal want Rosalind here?" my mother asked.

"Well, the police, some of them, think he's either throwing his weight around because she caught him stealing . . . or else . . . there's the possibility he's interested in Julie."

"Not *that* interested," my mother said. "I don't believe it."

"Thank you, Ann. I don't either. . . . I've known some of the girls Neal has fancied. What does he want with this undeveloped child?"

"How do *you* know Julie's undeveloped?" I snapped.

Mom said, *"Edgar."*

"From your photographs of her!" the doctor barked.

"Oh, sinful, sinful photographs!" I said.

"They weren't innocent photographs," said the doctor.

"Migawd!" I said.

"Honey?" Mom said. "Easy."

The doctor took another swig of wine and this time swished it around in his mouth as though it was Listerine and he was about to gargle. "This is an inferior Merlot," he said.

"It's fine, Darwin."

"Not for thirty-five dollars it isn't!" he said. Then he went back to the subject. "Rosalind says her niece has always felt left out, because she's always *been* left out. According to Rosalind this child desires to lose . . . and others sense that she is one of life's losers. They shun her."

"Rosalind may be thinking of her own childhood," said my mother.

"God forbid that she think of those days!" he said, as though he'd been there.

"Julie doesn't desire to lose!" I said.

The doctor was ignoring my fury and continuing. "From the time of her unmarried mother's unfortunate accident, she was left unclaimed by whatever relatives there were . . . and after Rosalind very kindly adopted her, she was shunned by classmates, dismissed from boarding schools, and even here in Serenity *friendless* except for the one friend I saw to it she had."

I hadn't told Mom about that. I'd wanted her to keep on thinking we'd been asked to Peligro because of her.

Mom sighed. "I was so flattered, too, that a woman like

Mrs. Slaymaster would want me to do an astrological chart. I felt very gullible when you finally told me why we were really asked to Peligro."

"You're not gullible, Ann. It's just that Rosalind is a trifle manipulative. She's had to be, to make her way."

"Bullshit!" I said under my breath. "And I'm not her only friend! Neal is her friend too!"

"Let's talk about something else," said Mom.

"*D'accord,*" said The Quack. "Let's."

So for a while they talked about a paper the doctor was presenting at some conference in Philadelphia. Something to do with what makes an optimist . . . which reminded me of the chicken poem . . . which made me doubt that The Duck knew anything about optimism.

He had polished off his whole steak while I was only about a third through and asking for a doggy bag. He was resting his elbows on the arms of his chair, holding his hands protectively around the Phi Beta Kappa key strung across his vest. He was eyeing me, like some district attorney on a TV series.

"And what is *your* fascination with Julie Slaymaster, E.C.? Do you mind my asking?"

"Yes."

"What do you mean 'yes'?"

"I mean I mind you asking."

"They're soulmates of sorts," my mother said.

"That's a good way to put it," I said.

"What are soulmates?" the doctor asked.

"A soulmate," my mother said, "is someone you have possibly crossed time to be with."

"I don't know about *that*," I said.

"You two have had a lot of happy hours at Peligro, haven't you?" Mom said.

"Who wouldn't like spending time *up there*?" The Duck said, before I could answer.

"You should know," I said.

He sat back, opened his coat, and let his belly hang out.

"Someone once wrote that innocence is like a dumb leper who has lost his bell. . . . You and your pal don't know what you've done here. Maybe you, personally, E.C., didn't have anything to do with the dollnaping, but then again . . ."

"Then again what?" my mother said.

"Then again maybe E.C. is not the great *watcher* Rosalind seems to think he is." He looked directly into my eyes, a look that back in therapy made me imagine all there was for me to do was admit everything he already knew about me.

He said, "Your father was a journalist and a photographer, but you couldn't call him a watcher, could you, E.C.?" He didn't wait for my answer. He said, "Your father had an agenda, always. He was out to save the underdog."

"What are you saying, Darwin?" Mother asked.

"Maybe E.C. isn't that fascinated with Julie Slaymaster. Perhaps it's just a genetic instinct to save the underdog."

I hoped my face wasn't as red as I thought.

Mom said, "Did you ask us to dinner so you could accuse E.C. of taking Peale?"

"I haven't accused him of anything!"

Mom said, "Why label people? Watchers, doers—it's so silly."

"No sillier than Gemini, Pisces, Leo, and all the other names *you* have for people!"

I knew they were heading for a fight.

That was my opportunity to get out of there without having to comment on his remark about my having a genetic instinct to save the underdog.

Neal once said about Duke: He always pretends to be a bigger fool than he is. But it wasn't *that*, I didn't think, as much as it was that he was smart in only one way: professionally. He was plenty smart that way . . . but the rest of him was myopic.

"Mom? Should I leave now and take Doon for a walk?"

"Yes, honey. Good idea!"

"Doctor Duke? When you go to Peligro, will you please tell Julie I think of her? A lot."

I'd pushed my chair back and was about to stand when he said, "This theft of Peale is breaking Mrs. Slaymaster! She's being destroyed! Julie will be destroyed along with her!

That child won't make it on a ranch, in the middle of no-where, with no one for company but the workers and her aunt! And her aunt is practically"—his voice rose and the last three words were shouted in a voice cracking with emo-tion—"A BASKET CASE!"

Then *he* pushed *his* chair back and excused himself from the table.

The *Fast Copy* crew was dancing.

The waitress brought me the doggy bag, and I said, "As soon as he comes back, I'm leaving. Okay, Mom? You two are going to dance anyway."

"Not to this music," she said. "Yes, go, E.C. You're get-ting on each other's nerves tonight. . . . He's more upset than I've ever seen him."

"It's because of me," I said. "He's got it in for me."

He can read my mind, I thought. Why not? I poured my soul out to him right after Dad died. He knows what I think of him trying to fill Dad's shoes! . . . And now he probably knows I've got Peale.

"It isn't you, E.C. Don't you know what it is?"

"No, I don't. He doesn't give a damn about Julie!"

"It isn't Julie, either. Darwin is afraid of losing Rosalind Slaymaster." Mom's voice broke. She said, "He's in love with her, E.C. I don't think he even knows it himself."

"I'm sorry," I said.

"You were never that fond of him anyway, were you?"

"What's the difference?"

She let out a sigh that seemed to punctuate the end of something. She sat very still for a moment, looking at the dancers gyrating to 808 State but not seeing them, I was sure.

I was never able to admit that her feelings for him were that deep.

She looked over at me and said, "Doon needs a walk badly, E.C. Don't wait for Darwin to come back to the table."

I gave her a kiss and took off.

As I was leaving the dining room, the doctor was heading out of the men's, across to the *Fast Copy* table. He was all smiles, with one hand out, introducing himself.

Twenty-five

I tried to hitch a ride home, but nobody would stop for me.

I jogged, wanting to sort out my thoughts, trying to tell myself I didn't have to do what I *did* have to do.

It was a bright, mild, moonlit night. I felt as though I was running in a flood of stage light, the camera's eyes on me, the one eye that didn't weep watching me.

I tried to tell myself what I was going to do before that night was over, I was going to do because of what Darwin Duke had said about Julie visiting Serenity . . . and about Neal being let off if Peale was returned, and maybe . . . maybe, Neal could see Julie too, in the far future.

But I knew what Mrs. Slaymaster's promises were worth, if you could call them that.

I knew, too, that my grand plan for keeping Julie in Serenity was a total bust.

What good did it do to have Julie here, when we couldn't see each other, when she wasn't free to come and go or even e-mail and phone? And when the one person she wanted most to see was locked up.

I hadn't saved her. I'd just put her in limbo, and my best friend was in jail without bail, not really because of what he'd stolen from Peligro, but because of Mrs. Slaymaster's and the Serenity police's conviction he had Peale.

As I ran along the canal and up the street to our house, I knew exactly where I was going to take Doon for his walk. I wondered if the one responsible for where I was going knew, too.

Wasn't that the whole point of dinner at The Canal House—"my treat"?

It would be a long walk from my house to Peligro, particularly with Doon on the leash and Peale in my arms. But it would never be long enough to suit me, for I could not imagine what Fate had in store for me once I appeared there and confessed everything.

When I thought of Mrs. Slaymaster, I thought of those cold green eyes and I jogged faster, with my heart pumping from both the run and the fear in me.

I knew what real dread was, like some character out of a Stephen King book.

"Hey, Doon! Doon!" I shouted when I got in the house. "C'mon, fellow! We're going for a walk!"

No Doon. I wondered if he wasn't coming because my frightened voice made me sound loopy and hyper. Dogs always know when someone's off.

Arbus was sitting on the kitchen counter washing her left back leg. I stuck the doggy bag in the refrigerator.

"Where's Doon?" I said to her. She didn't bother glancing in my direction, just changed legs and continued lapping away at her fur.

Something was wrong. Doon always came running the second the front door opened. And he could hear the door to the refrigerator from way out in the backyard.

My heart began hammering even harder, and I thought of Mom saying she'd had this feeling all day that something was going to happen.

I began looking under and behind furniture. Doon hid when he was sick or guilty.

I could just barely see him way back behind the couch.

Near him something sparkled in the light from the table lamp.

Sometimes when he was left too long without his walk, he found ways to push open things, to root under things, to jump up and get things. Then whatever he came upon he ripped apart and chewed up.

But Doon would never have swallowed anything like one of Peale's green glass eyes.

—from *THE SERENITY BANNER*
SUNDAY BOOK SECTION

INTERVIEWER: Rumor has it that you were actually involved in the doll-naping. Do you care to comment?

AUTHOR: Yes, I was the real dollnaper, and it was my Airedale who chewed the thing to pieces. I had to go to the place I call Peligro with what was left of it in a paper bag.

INTERVIEWER: What came next?

AUTHOR: One of the twin brothers was at the door, and he wasn't going to let me in until I told him that I knew where the doll was. Then I was inside, and Rosalind Slaymaster was coming toward me. The first thing I thought was that she'd shrunk, for she was always someone I had to look up to. But I realized she wasn't standing up straight. Her shoulders were slumped. Her white shirt was stained. I had never seen her when she didn't look immaculate. Then the strangest thing . . . (Author pauses and takes a long drink of water).

Then the strangest thing. When she asked me if I knew where

Peale was, she could hardly get his name out. She kept going Puh, puh, puh, puh . . . and I realized that she was stammering.

Well . . .

INTERVIEWER: Would you like to take a break? We've been at this for an hour and a half.

AUTHOR: No, let's get it over with. . . . I couldn't bring myself to hand the paper bag to her. It was the kind my mother put my lunch in on school days. There was not enough left of the doll to fill it. Doon had chewed up most of him.

"Peale is gone," I managed to say.

I thought she would pull my arm out of my socket. "Gone where? Where did you leave him?"

Then Julie appeared.

INTERVIEWER: The niece.

AUTHOR: Yes. She said, "Aunt, let me talk to him."

Mrs. Slaymaster stepped back, as though she would do just about anything now if she thought it would bring him back. She was smoking no hands, and pacing around the marble floor where that past Christmas Eve I'd seen her in a long gown, dancing with her doll, singing their song.

I remember wishing in that tiny second of time we could all go back to then, begin all over, all of us and the doll.

"*You* didn't take Peale, Eddie," Julie said in this soft voice that someone would use to calm down a confused mental patient. "Don't take the blame for Neal. You *said* he was diabolic, that he could play dirty: Well, he did. . . . Just tell us where Peale is."

I handed the paper bag to her.

While she looked inside it, I said that I was sorry, that Doon had done it.

I had never seen such an expression on her face. There was enormous sadness in that look, but there was a strength, too, almost as though she suddenly realized that she was the only one who could take charge now of this undreamed-of horrible situation.

Then, without warning, Mrs. Slaymaster grabbed the bag, like a street thief stealing a purse, and she took it to the small entrance table where there was a vase of fresh flowers and an ashtray in the shape of a horseshoe.

She left her cigarette smoking in the ashtray, then emptied the bag on the marble surface.

I believed that I would hear her scream for the rest of my life.

Twenty-six

The traffic that poured into Serenity that May day was all due to Sonny. It was one of the sleekest amusement parks in the northeast, nothing at all like it used to be when it was Dutchman Park.

The town council had seen to it that its construction was under way and over quicker than emergency housing for a disaster, all because it was feared Mrs. Slaymaster would sue to have her money returned, since she no longer planned to live among us.

Neal and I had both gone to the enormous yard sale at Peligro, and he had bought the iron horse's head attached to the mailbox, which had been there when the Evanses owned the place.

In a pile of old books I'd recognized the scrapbook I had

flipped through New Year's Eve, along with the diaries. They cost me $10. I never told Neal what I'd read about his father in them, never even hinted that Perry Kraft had figured so much in Rose Fitch's life. *Maybe it wouldn't help him to know all that* became my excuse for keeping it secret. Maybe it was better that he knew only what his mother had told him.

Probably I was avoiding confrontation, the way Mrs. S. said I did—afraid Neal'd do something rash, go to the ranch, make a scene—who knew what Neal would do?

I'd put everything in our basement, remembering, as I did, that Peale's green cashmere sweater was stuffed into a rug there.

I'd taken it out. It had still smelled faintly of Tommy. All of it had gone into a suitcase.

Neal and I went up to Sonny for the grand opening, complaining all the way, like most natives, finding fault with everything. It was a glitzy wonderland that would bring tourists to Serenity by the busload.

Inevitably, whenever Neal and I were together, we talked of Julie. We imagined how offensive she would find the place, what she would say about it ("gross!" and in Slutspeak "hideo"). It was a desperate attempt to keep her in our lives.

We sat on a Sonny Fitch Park bench munching hot dogs across from what was once The Sleepy Lagoon. Now it was called Wild Waters, and inside there were supposed to be faux ghouls and alligators, sea snakes and zombies.

We could hear the screams from customers in Wild Waters, and after a while we heard a familiar voice. "You boys mind company for a bit?"

Neal shrugged, and I moved down to make room.

The Duck managed a small smile and sat beside me.

"What's the word from The Lucky Star?" I said. I knew he'd helped them move back to Texas and that he visited there. He called Mom sometimes to cry on her shoulder.

"Are you asking about Julie?" he said.

"Yes, sure."

"She'll go to school there in the fall. She's been helping Rosalind." Then he corrected it to "Mrs. Slaymaster," as if her first name wasn't fit for our hooligan ears.

"What does she do?" Neal asked. "Does she work around the ranch?"

The doctor shot Neal one of those looks it's claimed would kill if looks *could*. He said his words very slowly. "Do you understand that losing Peale, for Mrs. Slaymaster, was the same as losing *you* would be for your mother?"

"I just asked what she *did*," said Neal. "I can't imagine Jewel on a ranch."

"*Jewel!*" said the doctor sarcastically. "What 'Jewel' *does* is care for her aunt. Her aunt is an emotional plane crash! You would not know that Rosalind Slaymaster is the same woman you boys saw looking so glamorous last Christmas Eve. . . . Where did you get those hot dogs?"

"You want me to get you one?" Neal asked.

"If you feel inclined," said The Duck.

When Neal was gone, the doctor took out his handkerchief, a red plaid job with DCD stiched in white across one corner. He wiped his forehead.

He said, "All the wind is out of her sails, that poor woman. Julie does everything now. She did from the moment they arrived at the ranch. She had to see to all the funeral arrangements herself."

"*Funeral* arrangements?"

"There was a big funeral for Peale. He had a lot of friends in Texas. There was a party after, at the ranch, for two hundred guests. Julie had to do everything Rosalind would have done."

"Don't you think Mrs. Slaymaster will get over it eventually?"

The doctor looked at me as though I'd asked him if it was safe to swallow Lysol. He said, "She will *never* be all right again! You don't seem to appreciate the fact that Peale was more than a talisman. . . . The end of Peale was the end of her best times, and her best times were all the more dear, for they were a long time coming. . . . The great pity is that she does not want anyone around to remind her of Peligro *or* Serenity. Not anyone."

"Including you?"

"I'm afraid so. . . . We were just beginning to relate on a remarkably deep level last winter, which is what is so disheartening about it."

"Too bad," I managed.

"Remarkably deep," said he, shaking his head sadly. "And now all that is kaput. Why, I had every intention of asking Rosalind, *Mrs.* Slaymaster, if your mother and I could be married at Peligro."

"What?" I cried.

"Oh, didn't your mother mention that we'd talked about it?"

"No, she didn't."

"Of course, Ann was jealous of Rosalind, *Mrs.* Slaymaster, but we were just very close, deep companions."

He let out a long sigh and then turned to me, swinging one fat little leg up on the bench. "I gave Julie—why does Neal call her Jewel, as though she were some fan dancer? I gave Julie your best wishes, as your mother asked me to do. In the last telephone conversation I had with them, she inquired about you and Neal."

"Why didn't you call me and tell me?"

"Because she said not to. Julie's best bet now is to mind her aunt, who doesn't fancy you *or* Neal!" His face had turned pink bordering on red. "For *very good* reason!"

230

"Okay." I didn't want to get him going.

"No, not okay," he said. "Nothing is okay."

Neal returned with three hot dogs.

"I can't eat that many," said The Duck.

"E.C. and I are having seconds, so there's one apiece."

We sat there for a while eating and talking about the park, the doctor grumbling that he was quite sure Mrs. Slaymaster had left explicit instructions that it be called *Sonny Fitch* Park.

"It does say that on the sign at the entrance," said Neal.

It said other things too, graffiti rhyming with Fitch.

"But look around you," said the doctor. "The vendors are all wear hats just saying Sonny. The buses have Sonny on their front cards. The balloons say it."

The doctor finished his hot dog and brought the plaid handkerchief out again to wipe his hands.

He slid forward so his feet reached the ground.

"I don't blame you boys," he said. "You may think I do, but I don't."

"For what?" Neal said.

He looked at Neal and said, "For *your* theft of the silver, which of course was a catalyst of sorts." Now his glance fell on me. "Or for *your* theft of Peale."

Neither Neal nor I would ever convince anyone that we hadn't worked in tandem. Only our mothers believed us.

He repeated, "I don't blame you."

I knew Neal was about to say something sarcastic, so I hit his side with my elbow, and we waited for what would come out of Wo-o-o Feelings' mouth next.

"Where I place the blame," said the doctor, "is on that damn little leather doll!"

"Ex doll," said Neal.

"I'm perfectly serious," The Duck said. "That piece of leather wasn't lucky! It was a jinx! It didn't grant wishes, it destroyed them! Rosalind, *Mrs.* Slaymaster, said that doll was why she adopted Julie, and that child has brought nothing but trouble to her aunt! Then, too, if it weren't for Peale, I think Ann and I would be back together. But his theft threw us *all* out of whack!"

Another big sigh.

I felt like saying at least the worst scenario—*me* living under the same roof with *you*—is no longer a possibility. But that thought only led to the other side of the coin: Julie, banished to the ranch with her aunt, out of my reach and my life.

The Duck gave us a little two-finger salute and said, "Good-bye, boys. Enjoy your day."

"Good-bye, sir," said Neal.

"*Sir?*" I said under my breath.

"The poor bastard! I can remember when I used to think

how smart he was. Now he's pathetic."

"He's both," I said.

We finished our dogs and walked along, listening to some mariachi music up by the Bullfighters' Ring. I remembered Julie telling us New Year's Eve about a party her aunt had given with mariachi music and piñatas. She was the only kid there. . . . I supposed she'd be the only kid there for a long time to come, and I couldn't think about it without wondering if I was going to puke.

Neal said, "Notice he says Rosalind, *Mrs.* Slaymaster, but he doesn't say Ann, *Mrs.* Tobbit. . . . Do you think he was in love with that woman?"

"Mom thinks he still *is*. Mom says if all this had never happened, she could have married him and never known he was drooling over Rosalind, *Mrs.* Slaymaster."

"What I don't understand," Neal said, "is how people get attracted to the people they get attracted to. . . . How does it happen? It can't be sex appeal. Your mother couldn't have been turned on by Dr. Duke. Like me. I wasn't turned on by Julie, but I can't get her out of my head."

"But my mother *was* turned on by him," I said. "I just couldn't admit it."

"I can't believe that, Easy."

"Believe it! And Peale *did* bring luck! If Doon hadn't chewed him up, Mom could be married to The Duck."

Neal said, "He brought luck to you, but what about Julie?"

"Don't," I said.

That night when I got home, I reread the letter Julie had written me the day she left, telling myself it would be the last time.

> *Dear Eddie,*
>
> *I was (still am) flabbergasted to know you could lie so coolly. If it had been Neal, I'd have thought now I'll tell one, but I honestly believed that you knew nothing about Peale's disappearance.*
>
> *The only thing I can do now is pray that Aunt snaps out of the funk she's in. Then maybe next year I could go to that school she's always raving about, Le Rosey, which would be better than life here in the hills with the four kinds of deadliest snakes just outside the door. (Honest!) Knowing you was like a dream— we were so easy together. And Neal was the dream come true. Only the dream didn't last. Dreams don't.*
>
> *I don't want to hear from you after this. Don't screw me up by making an appearance in my mailbox, on my e-mail, over our phone, fax, and God forbid in person. . . . Aunt is just barely coming around, and you could ruin everything again.*

The "again" was crossed out.

I've written Neal the same thing.

Enjoy your life, Eddie. Don't you wonder how everything will turn out?

Love,
Julie

P.S. Don't blame yourself.

I put Julie's letter in the suitcase with the diaries, the scrapbook, and Peale's green cashmere sweater. Why was I saving them? I wondered. What for?

Twenty-seven

Julie Slaymaster never left my thoughts. She was there in the same way someone is who's died, and you find yourself thinking of her more than you ever did when she was alive.

Even after I left Serenity and went off to the University of Pennsylvania, she was on my mind. Particularly at night when it was quiet and dark. I was afraid that I had ruined her life. I would go over everything, trying to believe that her exile in Texas was not my fault.

Again and again on campus, and in Philadelphia, I imagined that I saw her. But colleges and big cities are like that: filled with young girls who look like ones you've known from somewhere, sometime.

At the end of my junior year I took a course called "Writing the Memoir." I wasn't even sure I wanted to be a writer anymore, but by writing about Julie, I kept her close at the same time I let her go. I had intended to have it be Julie's story, but Mrs. Slaymaster began to impose herself on what had turned into a novel.

I would go back and forth between the two, always confounded by Julie, trying to imagine her life.

I longed for the strangeness of them. I looked around my life for someone even slightly off center. Neal had long since stopped trying to be different and now wore clothes from Abercrombie and Paul Stuart.

I would remember things like Julie in The Package Room wrapping Peale's blazer so he could go on a hunt. I'd laugh to myself over how easy it became to believe that doll was alive. I missed the music and the movies at Peligro, all the luxuries of life there, but mostly I missed the screwiness of them. It was as though they were inhabiting a Diane Arbus photograph and for a while had invited me in to live there, too.

Senior year during Christmas vacation I went for a hike with Neal. He was running KDS, and he had bought a small bungalow up on the cliffs overlooking the canal.

"You'll never guess who's in town," he said. "Our old girlfriend, Julie Slaymaster."

We were already on the trail, and I wondered why he hadn't told me in the car, on the way there.

"They say she's moving back to Peligro," Neal said. "You know they call it Eagle Rock now?"

"Yes. What took you so long to tell me she's here?"

"I forgot, E.C. Migawd, how long has it been?"

"Six years. How could you forget Julie?"

"I didn't mean that I forgot her totally. She's not on my mind like she's on yours. Are you still trying to write that book?"

"Trying. Right. Did her aunt buy back the place? Was she with her aunt?"

"Whoa! Hold on, E.C. My mother told me she's here. I didn't see her."

"Who said she's going to live at Eagle Rock?"

"It's some rumor floating around."

I wouldn't have known Julie if I had come upon her at Penn or in Philadelphia.

Her hair was cut short in a smart, blunt style. Without glasses her eyes were a very light blue, and the freckles seemed to have disappeared. She had a certain glow about her face, a tan maybe, or makeup, for she appeared quite glamorous.

I thought she had grown taller, but when I looked down, I noticed she was wearing high-heeled boots with a long, black skirt, and a black belted coat with a high collar. Around her neck there was a black-and-white silk scarf.

She was all smiles.

"Hello, Eddie."

We were at The Rainbow Diner, one of the few local places Mrs. Slaymaster had mentioned in her diary that were still there.

"You look lovely, Julie. I wouldn't have recognized—" I stopped myself, and she jumped in to rescue me.

She said, "I've changed. I know. People do in seven years."

"Six," I said.

"It's been seven years, Eddie. . . . But *you* don't look that different."

She had paid her check and was standing by the cash register. I had just arrived, on my way to the counter for a cup of coffee while I waited for Crowning Glory to close.

That night my mother and my stepfather and I were going to Bookworm, where he was reading from his new biography of Tycho Brahe, the astronomer.

I thought of inviting Julie to join us. I would have loved nothing better, but I was afraid that maybe too much time had passed for me to act on impulse. Probably from Rosalind Slaymaster's point of view too little time had passed for the likes of me to ask her niece out.

I could wait. I would, too. I kept thinking: Look at her!

"Julie, someone told me you and your aunt were moving back to Peligro?"

"Aunt died four years ago, Eddie."

"There wasn't anything in *The Banner* about it. Mom would have told me."

"It didn't make the papers. Aunt said she didn't want to give people any satisfaction." Julie grinned. "You know how she was. But didn't people notice the rents weren't going up?"

"I've been away," I said. "I'm at Penn."

"*I* bought Peligro. I loved it there, you know. Did you know that?" She ducked her head to look up at me with a mischievous smile. "Remember the chicken poem? I *was* that chicken."

She was looking all over my eyes, and I had to remind myself it was Julie and not someone new. I felt such a pull toward this woman, and there was no doubt that was what she had become. At twenty-two she was no longer a girl, as some still were.

"Will you be living here full-time or part-time in Texas?"

"Part-time on The Lone Star. I got to like the ranch . . . and maybe you know that I spent a year in Switzerland?"

"Whatever you've been doing, it agrees with you, Julie. You look just beautiful."

"What a sweet thing to say, E.C. You have to come to Peligro."

"Are you going to call it that again?"

"I never called it anything else," she said. "We should be all settled in by spring. Should I give a party? Do you get time off from school then?"

I knew that I was grinning and nodding, and probably my face was red and shiny with excitement. It took me a while to hear the "we" that had been squeezed into the conversation.

"We?" I asked finally.

"My husband and I. I'm Julie Parla now. I never was a very convincing Slaymaster."

I felt that news like a small, soft punch to my gut, covered by a big smile directed at her big smile.

"I was going to write you and thank you, Eddie."

"For what?"

"If you hadn't taken those photographs, and then Peale, I would have kept going to stupid schools, trying to force my way into little hicky cliques like The Sluts. I was some mess, wasn't I?"

I was about to guess, and then ask, which twin it was she'd married, when I saw him coming out of the men's, heading our way very slowly. I think he saw us, too. He was taking his time, looking down.

I would have probably guessed Diego, the sun, the smiler, Dr. Jekyll, but of course she'd chosen Paulo, the night, Mr. Hyde. Little mustache. Scowl.

I had to remind myself her favorite songs and books and movies were about the ones who had more reason to scowl than to smile. I could almost see that chicken among the stacked crates, with her head hanging between the bars of the cages, trying to see beyond the car following the truck.

I choked out congratulations.

Paulo stepped up, not scowling, nor smiling, either.

We shook hands and he said he remembered me, but I was sure that after we parted, Julie'd have to tell him I was the one who took Peale.

He put his arm around Julie while she told me they had sold most of the acreage of "Aunt's ranch," but Diego was managing what was left.

She laughed. "You should see him now. He's a real cowboy."

There was a pause. I wondered if she'd ask about Neal. She didn't, so I said, "I took a hike with Neal just yesterday."

"How is Neal?"

"He's made a real success out of KDS."

"Neal was a born entrepreneur," Julie said. "Tell him I'm going to have a party when spring comes."

After some small talk they wished me Merry Christmas and left. I watched them go to the sleek Porsche I'd noticed when I'd pulled into the parking lot. I'd wondered then who it belonged to. It was new.

They seemed new, too. I didn't know how long they'd been married, but they had that way about them some newlyweds have, touching each other more than other people do, walking close together.

When I'd left Penn for Christmas vacation, I had stopped working on the novel. I had come to the part where my hero was agonizing about whether he had caused great damage to the girl and, as a result, to himself as well.

The old mantra was ringing in his head. What became of her? What became of her?

After she left, I drank some coffee and remembered Christmases gone by, always sad for me no matter where I was or who I was with. I would recall that Christmas at Peligro, see myself at the party in the solarium, sitting with Julie, the brilliant blue kilifish swimming behind us. That was when it had begun, and although we had not known each other for very long, I'd come to believe that if we'd never met, her life would be quite different.

And so it would be . . . just not as I'd feared.

That spring I finished the novel, working on it at Penn during intersession instead of going home.

In the summer, back in Serenity, I began sending it off to agents and publishers who'd answered my inquiry, asking them if they would have a look.

Thanks to Sonny, we were growing into a real summer vacation spot, and locals learned to avoid town. We spent a lot of time in our own houses and yards, counting the days until "they" left.

There was a party at Peligro on the Fourth of July, with everyone in town invited. It was a benefit for Tall Trees.

Neither Neal nor I went. We'd already watched the fireworks from those windows. We imagined it would be crowded there and that there'd never be a chance to talk with Julie.

But a few times that summer, when I was on that road at night, I'd slow down and look up at Peligro. I'd remember the three of us when we were younger. I'd see the reflection of the moon in the river, and hear the music again, coming from the top of the hill.

ABOUT THE AUTHOR

M. E. Kerr is a winner of the American Library Association's Margaret A. Edwards Award for Lifetime Achievement. She lives in East Hampton, New York. The real-life model for Peale is buried nearby in a Sag Harbor cemetery beside the large white tombstone of his mistress.

Ms. Kerr's web site is http://www.columbia.edu/~MSK28/